Mother Courage

Mother Courage

JOHANN VON GRIMMELSHAUSEN

TRANSLATED BY WALTER WALLICH

LIFT-GROUND DRAWINGS BY FRITZ WEGNER

THE FOLIO SOCIETY · LONDON

1965

PRINTED IN GREAT BRITAIN

Printed by Richard Clay (The Chaucer Press), Ltd, Bungay

Set in "Monotype" Plantin 11 point, leaded 1 point

Bound by W & J Mackay & Co Ltd, Chatham

Contents

Translator's Introduction

Hans Jakob Christoffel von Grimmelshausen (*ca* 1622–76) was the father of the modern German novel and influenced it as profoundly as Defoe did the English novel a few years later. But though he towered head and shoulders above his contemporaries and, unlike Defoe, found no immediate and worthy successors, we knew until recently remarkably little about his life and person, and even today our knowledge is far from complete.

To some extent this ignorance reflects the troubled times into which Grimmelshausen was born—the Thirty Years' War which ravaged Germany from 1618 to 1648, decimating the country's population and destroying its towns and villages. Not many public and private records survived the holocaust, and most Germans who try to trace their family trees find that the thread breaks off at or about this period.

But another reason why we know so little about Grimmelshausen is undoubtedly his practice of writing under a bewildering array of pen-names, all of them anagrams of his own. Here are a few samples: Melchior Sternfels von Fugshaim, Philarchus Grossus von Trommenheim, Signeur Messmahl, Simon Lengfrisch von Hartenfels, Erich Stainfels von Grufensholm; and there are a number of others. Why he did this we do not know. Some say it was because literature in those days was held in abject contempt in Germany; others because he was describing contemporary events and feared to offend some of the protagonists in his books who were still alive.

Whatever the reason, the result was that for more than a century after his death men of letters were still attributing his books to imaginary authors, and when they finally stumbled on the truth many of the clues to Grimmelshausen's life had vanished for ever.

During the past half century, however, painstaking research has unearthed many facts which provide us with a fairly coherent picture of the novelist's life. He was born in the small town of Gelnhausen, at the foot of the Spessart mountain in the province of Hesse, probably in 1621 or 1622. His family originally belonged to the landed gentry, but his grandfather and father, who seem to have been simple tradesmen in Gelnhausen—probably bakers or innkeepers—dropped the 'von', the prefix designating aristocratic descent, from their names. The novelist resumed it some time after his father's death. In 1634, when Grimmelshausen was about twelve or thirteen years old, Gelnhausen was sacked by the Croats and he was separated from his family and swept up by the army. What happened to him during the following years can be gathered in part from his most famous novel, *Simplicius Simplicissimus*, which is to a large extent autobiographical. Though fact and fiction are almost inextricably interwoven in it, it seems clear that for several years he drifted with troops, now of one side and now of the other, from one battle and siege to the next; first as a page or stable lad and later, when he grew up, as a soldier in his own right. We can deduce this, however, only from the special knowledge of historical events which he reveals in his novel. Records of his career during this period there are none.

The first documented news we have of him dates from the year 1639 when, at the age of eighteen or nineteen, he appears as a musketeer in the fortress of Offenburg, not far from Strasbourg, in the Principality of Württemberg. Six years later, in 1645, documents in his own hand show him to be established as a scribe or clerk in the orderly room of the Commandant of the fortress, Colonel Hans Reinhard von Schauenburg, where he remained at least until 1648, by which time he seems to have advanced to the position of secretary to one of the regiments quartered in the fortress. As such he would have ranked just above the regimental chaplain. For a soldier forcibly uprooted from his home and separated from his family at the age of twelve, and thereafter with little or no opportunity of formal education, a commendable career. He seems to have retired from this post when the regimental commander died in 1649 and his successor brought his own secretary with him.

The Thirty Years' War was now at an end. In 1649 Grimmelshausen married, in Offenburg, Catharina Henninger, a young
woman of good family and the daughter of an officer. They had
nine children, four sons and five daughters, most of them born
in Gaisbach, a village in the Black Forest and the seat of the
Schauenburg family, whose steward and agent he now became,
presumably through the good offices of Colonel von Schauenburg. He must have been about twenty-seven or twenty-eight
years of age when he took up his new post, and it was certainly
no sinecure. The Schauenburgs were important landowners
and documents show that he administered their estates, maintained and improved their buildings and conducted their
frequently complicated financial and legal affairs. Grimmelshausen served the Schauenburgs for eleven years, until 1660,
when he was given notice, seemingly because the family were
not altogether satisfied with his stewardship. During his time
with the Schauenburgs he also did some business on his own,
as a horse dealer and for three years—from 1655 to 1658—as
an innkeeper. He seems to have abandoned this enterprise as
suddenly as he took it up, why we do not know.

Grimmelshausen next spent three years—from 1662 to 1665
—as steward to a wealthy physician in the same district, and
then returned to Gaisbach for another two years, again as an
innkeeper. His establishment was called the Silver Star, and
does not seem to have been particularly successful, for by 1667
he was seeking new employment. He found it with the Bishop
of Strasbourg, who appointed him chief magistrate in the small
neighbouring town of Renchen in his diocese, where he remained until his death in 1676. He must then have been about
fifty-six years of age, and the entry in the parish register says
that all his family was gathered around him and he received
Holy Communion before he died. This, as well as his employment by the Bishop of Strasbourg, shows him to have been a
Roman Catholic. His birthplace, Gelnhausen, on the other hand,
was in a Lutheran part of Germany, and he was almost certainly born into the Lutheran confession. When he changed his

11

religious allegiance we do not know, but it may well have been at the time of his marriage.

We know little in detail about his activities during his time in Renchen, practically all the relevant documents having perished, but his duties, in so small a parish, are not likely to have been very onerous. Towards the end of his life, however, they must have been greatly complicated by invading French armies. The entry in the parish register referring to his death indicates that he had recently taken service again with the Imperial armies, probably on an emergency basis.

We have no portrait of Grimmelshausen, and anything we can say about his appearance is almost pure conjecture. Assuming, however, that the hero of his *Simplicius Simplicissimus* is modelled on the author physically as well as in other respects, we may regard him as having been unusually tall and broad-shouldered, for there are several references to Simplicius' great stature. The only other physical peculiarity at which we can make a guess is the colour of his hair and beard, which may have been red. The evidence for this consists of two small tracts in defence of red hair, one of them entitled: *Manifesto against Those who so peevishly and knavishly malign and persecute the Owners of Red and Golden Beards*. The tracts were evidently the outcome of some obscure personal feud, but from certain turns of phrase in them it seems likely that Grimmelshausen was one of those who were 'peevishly and knavishly maligned and persecuted'.

Grimmelshausen's writings all date from 1658 or later, that is to say from the period after he had settled in the Black Forest. He certainly would have had little time for writing, never mind publishing his works, during his wartime wanderings. The miracle is that with his rudimentary education he became a writer at all and so accomplished a writer at that. He presumably went to the Lutheran school in Gelnhausen at the age of six, as was the rule, and until the tides of war swept him away some six years later will have learned reading, writing and arithmetic according to his age, as well as a little Latin and a good deal of divinity. But even at best it cannot have been more than a very elementary education. His wanderings and service with the army will have taught him much practical wisdom and experience, and he may even have come into contact with men of culture, but of formal schooling there was almost certainly none. Yet his writings show him to have had an excellent knowledge of history, both ancient and contemporary, to have read widely in a number of languages, with a competent knowledge of Latin, Greek, French and Italian as well as a smattering of Hebrew, and to have had a more than passing acquaintance with medicine and alchemy. Finally, as steward to the Schauenburgs he must have been a competent accountant and something of an expert on agriculture and viniculture, and as magistrate of Renchen a passable lawyer. Also, as his writings reveal, he was a poet, philosopher and wit. All in all, then, a very remarkable man, and the more's the pity that he obscured his identity as a writer so effectively that despite the immediate and resounding success of his books we do not have a single personal account of him by a contemporary.

Grimmelshausen's first works were mainly conventional and derivative, satirical in intent but on the whole unremarkable. Then, in 1669, there appeared *The Adventures of Simplicius Simplicissimus, the Account of the Life of a strange Vagabond*, a novel about the Thirty Years' War, serious and bitingly satirical in content, yet sparkling with a robust and often crude humour. Though it was a picaresque novel and as such owed much to its Spanish and French models, its realism broke entirely new ground as far as Germany was concerned and it became an instant success with the public. Probably as a result, Grimmelshausen followed it up with a series of novels, short stories and tracts, collectively known as the Simplician Writings, featuring Simplicius and other characters from the first book. The main works in this series are *Courage, Happy-go-Lucky* and *The Miraculous Birds' Nest*, and of these *Courage* is probably the best known as well as the nearest in quality to *Simplicissimus*.

13

Its heroine provided the German playwright Berthold Brecht with the idea and name for his famous play *Mother Courage and her Children*, and though Brecht used none of the incidents from Grimmelshausen's novel the character of his Courage shares many traits with Grimmelshausen's creation.

Unlike *Simplicissimus*, *Courage* is in no way autobiographical, and Grimmelshausen did not even draw on his own experiences for the historic framework of the novel. He took it, instead, from two well-known contemporary German histories, and a comparison shows that he drew on them freely, even to the extent of verbatim accounts of battles, skirmishes and the movements of armies. Within this historical setting we can follow Courage's career in considerable chronological detail.

The battle of Budweis (Chapter II) was fought in September 1620. Courage was thirteen years old at the time, as she tells us, so this would place the date of her birth in 1606 or 1607.

The battle in which General Bucquoy was killed and the Captain of horse mortally wounded (Chapter IV) occurred in July 1621, so she was first married at the age of fourteen.

Her next two marriages—to the Captain of foot (Chapter VI) and to the Lieutenant with whom she came to blows (Chapter VII)—followed in rapid succession during 1622, the dates again fixed by two battles, Wisloch and Wimpfen, and the same year witnessed her exploits at the Main bridge (Chapter VIII).

There follows an interval of several years during which she left the army, sought out her old nurse and established herself in Prague. She married again (Chapter X) on the eve of the battle of Lutter (August 1626), but her husband was killed at the sack of Hoya in December of the same year (Chapter XI).

Her distressing experiences at the hands of her former captive (Chapter XII) and the short-lived idyll with the Danish nobleman (Chapter XIII) occurred during the first half of 1627, before she was abandoned in Hamburg at a time when 'Wallenstein, Tilly and Count Schlick descended on all Holstein . . . with a locusts' swarm of Imperial troops', which we know to have happened in the autumn of 1627.

The march of the three Imperial armies across the Alps into Italy (Chapter XV) occurred in the spring of 1629, and Courage's various exploits in Italy cover that and the following year. The armies, and Courage with them, were back in Germany by the autumn of 1630, and it was then that she cast Happy-go-Lucky adrift (Chapter XX).

She moved to Prague and contracted her fifth legal marriage (Chapter XXIII) some time after Wallenstein had taken the city and before the battle of Liegnitz, that is to say between 1632 and 1634. The description she gives of herself in this chapter would very well fit a young woman of between twenty-five and twenty-seven years.

Her encounter with Simplicius in Griesbach can be dated by textual comparisons of both books to 1640 or 1641. Simplicius would then have been about nineteen or twenty, and Courage thirty-four or thirty-five years old.

The battle of Herbsthausen, in which she lost her sixth husband, the musketeer (Chapter XXVI), occurred in 1645. Thereafter she joined the gipsies and stayed with them, as far as we know, for the rest of her life. A reference in Chapter II implies that she was sixty-three years old when she dictated her memoirs, which in turn tallies with the date of publication (1669) of *Simplicius Simplicissimus*, the reading of which, as she tells us, prompted her to set down her own reminiscences.

The motivation for this alleged riposte is not very convincing. In the sixth chapter of the fifth Book of his memoirs Simplicius gives us no more than the most cursory account of his meeting with Courage. His description of her is admittedly not very flattering, but he does not even mention her name, so that she could hardly complain that he had branded her publicly. In modern terms the passage would scarcely rate a libel action, and certainly does not seem to warrant all the expenditure of energy and spleen which Courage devotes to it. Perhaps it was the very fact that she rated no more than a paragraph in his reminiscences that riled her. Perhaps it was merely that Grimmelshausen needed some sort of a peg for his new novel.

But however slight the occasion which led Courage to dictate her own recollections (for we know from Chapter XVII that she did not write them herself), there is nothing half-hearted about the enterprise once she has embarked on it. She spares neither her own reputation nor her readers' susceptibilities. Indeed, some of the book must be as strong meat as was ever published in those days.

Though Grimmelshausen leads Courage, as he did Simplicius, through the Thirty Years' War in a series of picaresque adventures, the two are worlds apart as far as character is concerned. Simplicius is fundamentally a decent lad. His early pranks, however outrageous, are never vicious, and though in the long run the war corrupts and coarsens him, we are never left seriously in doubt as to his ultimate salvation.

Not so Courage. Though she has qualities of beauty, courage, intelligence and enterprise which would have won her success in almost any way of life, the times into which she was born, coupled with her strong sex drive and very feminine search for economic security—call it greed if you like—set her firmly on a course of moral abandon and delinquency. She is an accomplished and successful prostitute while still in her teens, and thereafter, as it were, never looks back until she takes the ultimate step into social degradation by becoming a gipsy. And it is no mean height from which she falls. Her nurse's account of her origins (Chapter X) as the daughter of a Count, until a few years ago the most powerful in the kingdom, but now banished and serving with the Turk, fits to perfection the historic figure of Count Heinrich Matthias von Thurn, who was born in 1580, rebelled against the Emperor in Prague in 1618, was banished after the battle of the White Mountain, spent some time in Constantinople and joined Bethlen Gabor in fighting the Emperor.

If from this rake's progress she nevertheless emerges as a rather lovable old reprobate it is largely because of her absolute spiritual and intellectual honesty. Not for her the moral hangovers which afflict Simplicius at the conclusion of some of his

16

more scurrilous escapades, or the lengthy moralizing in which he indulges as a result. She has no illusions about war—it tends to bring out the evil in men rather than the good, she says—but since these are the times in which she lives, she is determined to make the best of them, using them to amass a tidy fortune as a hedge against the leaner days of peace that may lie ahead. She is perfectly aware of the spiritual, moral and social perils which this conduct entails and faces them without rancour or self-pity. (It is this aspect of her character which Brecht singled out for the basis of his play.)

This fundamental difference between Courage and Simplicius Grimmelshausen has been brought out strikingly in the style of Courage's narrative. It is racy, direct and unpretentious. What few expressions of regret there are about her conduct are almost entirely concerned with lack of foresight which prevented her from arranging her affairs more judiciously. Her sorrow for the loss of even the two husbands she really loved—her seducer and the Captain who was killed at Hoya—is confined to a mere couple of lines. The only two people to whom she was linked by closer and more permanent ties—her nurse and Happy-go-Lucky—she exploits ruthlessly for her own ends, brazenly boasting of her success in corrupting them. The manner in which her complex relationship with Happy-go-Lucky emerges from the story without any conscious effort on her part and, indeed, without her even being aware of it, is entirely in keeping with her single-minded egotism and, incidentally, a touch of genius on Grimmelshausen's part. Here is a man so utterly besotted with love that he will consent to the most preposterous and humiliating conditions in order to be allowed to live with her. Predictably, it earns him nothing but contempt for his weakness. She seems quite heedless of the fires she has kindled and even expresses surprise at discovering him at her side in a church where she has gone to find herself a lucrative customer for the night. When at last he shows signs of breaking under the strain, first by taking to drink and gambling and then by trying to beat and murder her in his sleep (a fine and precocious psychological touch, this), her only reaction is fierce resentment and the immediate suspicion that he is after her money. She casts him adrift without a twinge of remorse, adding injury to insult by palming her dangerous familiar spirit off on him.

What, then, is her ultimate fate? Does wickedness reap its just reward? By no means. Grimmelshausen was too much of a realist for so sentimental a conclusion. A woman of Courage's energy, accomplishments and gifts does not readily go under in the struggle for life. Her introduction to the book shows her unrepentant to the point of effrontery, and a detailed description of her in a later volume of the Simplician Writings proves that though she may have lost social caste as a gipsy she continued to dominate her environment. The account is by the scribe to whom she dictated her memoirs, and it tells of his first meeting with her:

'A splendid gipsy woman, the like of whom I had never seen or heard of in my life, came riding up on a donkey. I took her for a Queen, or at the very least a Duchess among gipsies. She looked about sixty, but I have since calculated that she must have been somewhat older. In contrast to most of the other gipsy women, whose hair was jet black, hers was fair, and braided with strands of gold and jewels, with a small crown atop. Her complexion was still fresh and smooth, and to judge by her features she must have been a handsome woman in her youth. She wore earrings of filigree gold set with diamonds, and a pearl necklace which would have graced any Duchess. Her cloak was scarlet, lined with green velvet and adorned, like her skirt (which was of best English cloth), with a hem of silver braid. She wore no jerkin, and her blouse, of pure linen, was snow-white except for the seams which were embroidered with black silk after the Bohemian fashion, setting her off like a strawberry in a bowl of milk. On her feet she wore a pair of gay Polish leather boots, and her long gipsy knife she carried, not concealed under her skirt but openly, for it was a thing of beauty of which she might well be proud. All her companions called her "my lady", and to tell the truth, the old crone was a splendid sight on donkey-back (I had almost said horse-back) whose appearance has remained as vivid in my memory as it was on the day I met her.'

It is this same scribe who reveals to Simplicius the trick Courage played him by foisting on him her maid's child as her own. The news leaves him unruffled, for in this piece of double-dealing it is he who has the ace up his sleeve: 'Far from deceiving me,' he says, 'she did me a most valuable service. For while I was spooning with her I lay more often with her maid than with herself, and it pleases me much that my son, young Simplicius (whom I cannot disown since he resembles me so closely both in his character and his appearance), should have been born of the chambermaid rather than the wanton gipsy.'

W. W.

DEFIANCE TO SIMPLEX

or

Detailed and Most Strange

DESCRIPTION OF THE LIFE

of the Arch-trickster, Trollope and

Most Notorious Rogue

COURAGE

how first she became the wife of a Captain of horse,
then of a Captain of foot, then a pedlar,
a musketeer's wife and in the end a gipsy;
bravely and briskly told
and as pleasing, diverting and instructive to read
as 'Simplicissimus' itself.
The whole recounted by COURAGE herself,
in spite and defiance of the world-famous
Simplicissimus,
dictated by her to the author who for the nonce calls himself

PHILARCHUS GROSSUS VON TROMMENHEIM

OF GRIFFSBERG Etc.

PRINTED IN UTOPIA BY FELIX STRATIOT 1669

[*Note: The publisher has his own pseudonym, in fact.
His real name was Wolff Eberhard Felszecker, of Nuremberg*]

True origin and brief summary of this small tract

THE gipsy Courage, having read Simplicissimus' insolent description of her in the sixth chapter of the fifth Book of his memoirs, flies into a rage and determines to pillory him by the frank revelation of her infamous way of life. Nor does the fact that she thereby also betrays her own disgrace concern her in the least, for since joining the gipsies she has renounced all pretensions to honour and virtue. Her sole aim is to humble the said Simplicissimus before the eyes of all the world, by relating how lightly and heedlessly he succumbed to so coarse a slut as she professes herself to be (and is, indeed), and how he boasted of his wantonness and treachery to boot. From all of which she concludes that there is nothing to choose between the pot and the kettle, or a coxcomb and a whore, and that neither is better by one jot than the other. She also relates, with the utmost satisfaction, how cunningly she paid him back in kind for his treachery.

Chapter One

'INDEED!' you will say, my masters, 'Who would have thought the old beldam capable of trying to escape the imminent wrath of God at so late an hour? But needs must when the Devil drives. For the capers of her youth are over and done, her pride and lust have been laid low, her heavy conscience stirs guiltily within her, the onset of crabbed age disgusts her with the multitude of her former follies, and their secret memory fills her heart with loathing. The old carrion-crow senses that Death, stern and implacable, will soon be knocking at her door to serve her with the final writ for her journey to another world, where she will be summoned to account for all her exploits and misdeeds on this earth. And thence, no doubt, this most public attempt to relieve her old Adam of some of the crushing burden of her guilt, this endeavour to ease herself even at so late an hour towards the hope and prospect of divine mercy.'—Yes, my gracious masters, that is what you will say, or some of you at least.

Others again will wonder: 'Is Courage making a bold bid to repair and refurbish that raddled old hide which in her youth she pampered with French ointments, later daubed with all manner of Italian and Spanish fards, and at the last smeared with Egyptian grease and goose dripping as a protection against lice; that hide blackened by the smoke of so many camp fires, and so often scrubbed and tanned back to a semblance of its pristine pallor? Does she imagine that by thus unburdening and easing her heart of her manifold vices and knaveries she can smooth the ingrained wrinkles from her lewd brow and restore it to the sleek polish of its first innocence? Would the brazen old harridan, now that she has wellnigh both her legs in the grave (if, that is, she can find one to receive her), presume to make her peace with God?—She who wallowed all her life in every manner of shame and vice, who is burdened with more villainies than years, more whorings than months, more thefts than weeks, more mortal sins than days and more venial ones than hours, and who, old as she is, has never once given a thought to repentance? Does she believe there is still time, now that her conscience is beginning to torment her with more hellish pangs and twinges than ever in all her life she knew pleasures and delights of the flesh? Indeed, perhaps if this faded and useless fardel of Mother Earth had confined herself to the pleasures of the flesh instead of steeping herself as well in all manner of other vices and plumbing the very pit and bottom of evil; perhaps then she might yet entertain some faint hope of mercy in the life to come.'

That, my masters, is what you will say, that is what you will think, and these will be your expressions of amazement when you come to hear of this my Chief and Universal Confession. And I, when listening to you, will forget my age and laugh till I am young again or until I have shaken my very bones to pieces! 'And why, Courage? Why will you laugh thus?' many will ask. Because you imagine that an old woman who has enjoyed her life so long that her body and soul seem all of a piece would think of dying, that I, whom you know so well for what I am and

24

always have been, would consider repentance, or that one whose whole life—as every cleric will testify—has been so steadfastly directed straight to Hell could so belatedly start thinking of Heaven.

Let me say plainly that I have no mind to any such journey as the parsons would urge me to, for I am quite unable to comply with their chief demand, or to abandon those habits which they claim to be my worst impediments. Of one thing I have too little, and of several others—two in particular—I have too much. That which I lack is contrition; that of which I have too much is avarice and envy. If I hated the hoard of gold which I grubbed together at the risk of life and limb—and, they tell me, at the price of my salvation—as much as I envy my neighbour, and loved my neighbour as I do my gold, then, indeed, the heavenly gift of contrition might follow. Yet I know the different ages of woman and can confirm from my own experience that old dogs are rarely taught new tricks. My choler has grown with the years and I cannot cleanse myself of my bile like a butcher cleans a sow's stomach by turning it inside-out. So how can I tame my passions, and who is to bleed me of my long-pent-up phlegm and so cure me of my idleness? Who would rid me of the melancholy vapours that prompt me to envy? Who shall make me hate ducats when from long experience I know full well that they mean freedom from want and, perhaps, the only comfort of my old age? There was a time, my worthy parsons, for guiding me into the paths that now you would have me follow, when I was still in the flower of my innocence and the prime of my youth. For though even in those days I was assailed by lewd urges it would have been easier then to resist the call of the blood than it is now to combat the influence of the other three fluids—bile, phlegm and melancholy. Go, therefore, and seek out the young, whose hearts are not yet tainted, as mine is, with other images, and teach, admonish, exhort and implore them in order that they may never heedlessly go the way of poor Courage.

'But listen, Courage,' some may ask, 'if repentance is not

your aim, why then do you endeavour to tell your life's story in the guise of a confession, and reveal your vices to all the world?' I do it to spite Simplicissimus, because I have no other means of revenge. First, this insolent rascal got me with child at the waters in Griesbach, or so he thought. Then he rid himself of me by a cheap trick, and in the end he went forth and advertised his shame and mine to all the world by means of his famous memoirs. But in what follows I propose to show him what manner of woman it was with whom he dealt, so that he may know of whose conquest he boasted and wish, maybe, that he had held his tongue about it.

From all of which the esteemed public may gather that as a rule pots and pans, whores and coxcombs, are chips off the same block, and none so much as a whit whiter than the other. Deep calls unto deep, as the Devil said to the charcoal-burner, and sinners are mostly punished by sins and other sinners.

Chapter Two

THOSE who know how the Slav peoples treat their serfs might hazard a guess that I was begotten by a Bohemian nobleman upon a peasant's daughter. But there is a difference between guessing and knowing. I, too, may hazard a guess at this or that, yet I know it not, and if I were to say that I knew who were my parents I would be lying—nor, indeed, for the first time, either! But this I do know: that I was reared gently enough at Bragoditz, and was schooled and taught sewing, knitting and other such woman's work more carefully than would have befitted a common child. My board was paid regularly by my father, though I knew not whence, and my mother sent me many a token of her love, though I never exchanged a word with her.

When the Prince of Bavaria and General Bucquoy marched into Bohemia to drive out the new King, I was a pert girl of thirteen, just starting to wonder whence I came; and this was my most pressing concern, for I was not allowed to ask and could not discover it by other means. I was guarded from all commerce with my neighbours like a precious painting is protected from dust, and my nurse never let me out of her sight. So, since I was not permitted to play with other girls of my age, idle thoughts began to fill my mind with all manner of extravagant fancies which occupied all my waking hours.

When the Prince of Bavaria and Bucquoy split their forces,

the Prince moved against Budweiss and the General against Bragoditz. Budweiss wisely made haste to surrender, but Bragoditz held out and was made to suffer the full rigours of the Imperial arms, which showed such defiance scant mercy. My nurse, seeing how matters stood, came to me betimes and said: 'Maid Libuschka, if you would stay a maid you must needs have your hair shorn and put on men's clothing, for otherwise I would not give a shoe-buckle for your honour, which I am so earnestly charged to preserve.'—'What strange talk is this?' I thought, but she seized a pair of scissors and cut off my golden hair on the right side, leaving it long on the left—just as the nobles used to wear it in those days. 'And now, my daughter,' she said, 'if you come out of this business unscathed you will still have enough hair left for your adornment, and the rest will grow again within the year.' I was easily consoled, for from my earliest youth I have always been happiest when the times seemed most disordered. Then she dressed me in breeches and jerkin and taught me how to lengthen my stride and what movements and gestures were appropriate to my new station in life. And so we awaited the sack of the town by the Imperial troops, my nurse, indeed, with fear and trembling, but I looking forward eagerly to whatever strange and terrible events were to ensue. Nor did I have long to wait, but will not tarry here to tell how in a vanquished city the men are butchered, the women ravished and the town itself plundered; for these matters became so common and widely known during the late interminable war that all the world can tell a tale of it. This only must I mention if I am to give a true and faithful account of my life's story: that a German trooper took me with him as his lad, to mind his horses and to forage—that is to say, steal—for him. I called myself Janco, and though I had a fair command of German, like a true Bohemian I did not reveal it. For the rest, I was graceful of carriage, fair of face and gently mannered, and whoever today will not believe as much, I could but wish that he had seen me fifty years ago, when he would surely have given me a more favourable report.

When this my first master brought me to his company, his Captain, who was a handsome and brave young cavalier indeed, asked him what he intended to do with me. He replied: 'What troopers are wont to do with their lads; letting him mind my horse and steal for me, at which, by all accounts, the Bohemians excel. For it is said that a Bohemian will carry a bale of linen out of a house where a German, for sure, would not find so much as a spindle-full of flax.'—'And what,' the Captain retorted, 'if he began by practising his Bohemian skill on you and put it to the test by riding off with your horse?'—'Have no fear,' said the trooper, 'I shall keep a sharp eye on him until I have broken him in.'—'Peasant lads who have been trained with horses,' observed the Captain, 'make much better stable boys than town-bred striplings who have had no experience of the trade. Moreover, this lad seems to me well bred and much too tenderly reared to mind a trooper's mount.' At this I pricked up my ears most eagerly, though careful not to let them see that I understood any of their discourse, for they were speaking in German. My greatest concern was that they might chase me back to the sacked town of Bragoditz, for I had by no means had my fill yet of the sound of trumpets, drums, fifes and the thunder of guns, which had made my heart leap within me. In the end it was arranged (whether for good or ill I know not) that the Captain should keep me for himself, to wait upon his person as a page and servant. To the trooper—seeing that the fellow so much desired a thief of my race—he gave another raw Bohemian lad to mind his horses.

As for me, I played my part with a will and knew so well how to flatter my Captain, keep his clothes neat, his white linen spotless and to cosset him that he soon came to look upon me as the very paragon of a page. I also took a great delight in handling guns, and minded his so well that both master and servant could depend upon it at all times. So it did not take me long to prevail on him to give me a sword and to have me fitted out with a bandoleer. For all these qualities I was highly commended, and moreover soon regarded as marvellously quick-witted into the bargain for the speed with which I learned German, no one knowing that this had been part of my regular studies since earliest childhood. For the rest, I did whatever I could to disguise my womanish ways, diligently learned to curse like a trooper, drink like a brush-maker and pledge brotherhood with any ruffian whom I regarded as my equal. If I had occasion to swear by anything I did so with the coarsest and most brutish oaths I could muster, and all this I did in order to conceal what I had not been endowed with at birth and what, despite all outward appearances, I still lacked.

Chapter Three

MY Captain was (as I have already mentioned) a handsome
young cavalier, a fine horseman, a skilful fencer, a good dancer,
a gallant soldier and, above all things, a passionate hunter, ad-
dicted in particular to coursing. His face was as beardless as my
own, and if he had been attired in women's clothes he could
have passed without much difficulty for a pretty young maid.
But I digress and must return to my story.

After Budweiss and Bragoditz both armies marched on Pilsen, which held out bravely for a time but in the end suffered
the same punishment of slaughter and butchery as the others.
Thence they moved on to Raconitz, where I had my first taste
of a pitched battle. Then did I wish I were indeed a man, and
able to follow the wars all the days of my life, for we had so
merry an encounter that my heart leapt within me for joy. The

31

battle of the White Mountain, at the gates of Prague, further whetted my appetite, for our troops won a great victory and suffered but few losses. On that occasion my Captain made splendid booty, and as for me, I conducted myself not like a page or varlet, much less like a young girl, but rather like a true soldier who has sworn to meet the enemy in battle for a fair wage.

After this battle the Duke of Bavaria moved into Austria, the Elector of Saxony into Lusatia and our General Bucquoy into Moravia to subdue the rebels and restore them to the Emperor's allegiance. The General had been wounded at Raconitz, and while we rested to allow his hurt to be healed, my own heart was smitten by the kindness and favours I received from my Captain, for I heeded only those of his qualities that I have already mentioned, not minding in the least that he could neither read nor write and was so coarse a man that I can swear I never heard or saw him pray. And if Alphonso the Wise in person had called him a handsome beast it would not have quenched the fires of my love for him. The few remaining shreds of my maidenly modesty compelled me to keep this love a secret, but it burned so fiercely within me that despite my tender years, hardly fit yet for a man, I often yearned to take the place of those whom I and others brought to his bed from time to time. I was also, at first, strongly restrained from revealing my violent and reckless passion by the fact of my adored's noble and famous descent, and that most assuredly he would not marry a wench who did not even know her parents. As for becoming his mistress, this thought still repelled me at the time because of the many whores I saw daily selling their bodies to the troops.

Though sorely tormented by this fierce struggle within my heart, yet outwardly I was wanton and merry enough, and of so strong a constitution that neither my inner turmoil nor my hard work and the rigours of war affected me in any way. I had no other care than to tend my Captain, and this my love taught me to do with such zeal and diligence that my master would have sworn by all the saints that no more faithful servant ever trod this earth. In every skirmish, however brisk, I kept close to his side or guarded his back—though in truth it was none of my business—and never failed to find occasions to perform some task that would please him. Had not my apparel deceived him, he might well have guessed from the glances that I bestowed on him that I honoured and cherished him after a fashion quite unlike that of a common servant. Meanwhile my bosom grew apace and the shoe pinched me the longer the harder, until I feared I would soon be unable to conceal any longer either my outward appearance or my inward passion.

We went on to storm Iglau and take Trebitz, capture Znain and subdue Bruenn and Olmuetz, and bring most of the other towns under our sway, from all of which enterprises I received much booty, given to me by my Captain in return for my faithful services. I made good cheer with what I had, mounted myself splendidly, filled my purse and from time to time joined the troopers in downing a flagon of wine at the sutler's shop. It was at one of these revels that several of them who envied me my good fortune gave me hard words. One in particular taunted me, abusing and reviling the Bohemian nation beyond all reason. The coxcomb swore that some Bohemians had eaten a rotting dog full of maggots, which they had mistaken for an evil-smelling cheese, and he teased me about it as if I had been there in person. Over this we fell to scolding, thence to cuffing and scuffling, and at last to fighting and wrestling in earnest, when my adversary slipped his hand into my breech, trying to seize me by what I did not possess. This vain though murderously intentioned gesture enraged me far more than if it had achieved its purpose, and so embittered me as to drive me wellnigh out of my senses. I summoned all my strength and speed, and so scratched, bit, kicked and cuffed my assailant that in the end I gained the upper hand and scored his face with my nails until it looked more like a devil's mask than a human countenance. I would most likely have gone on to strangle him had not the rest of the company dragged me off and made peace between us. I

C 33

had suffered no more than a black eye, but suspected that the knave was now well aware of my true sex. And doubtless he would have revealed it there and then had he not feared either that it might earn him further blows or that he would be mocked for letting a girl beat him. Fearful that he might do it even now, if provoked, I turned on my heel and left the company.

My Captain was out when I returned to our quarters, having gone to make merry at a gathering of brother officers. There he heard of the fight I had had, even before I saw him. He liked me for the resolute young lad I was, and so did not take too grave a view of the offence, but he could not refrain from reading me a lecture about it. When, in the course of his sermon, he asked me why I had marked my adversary so cruelly, I replied that the fellow had tried to lay hold of me by my courage, which no man's hand had ever touched before (for I was reluctant to call it by the coarse word commonly used for those parts). Then, seeing that in any case my maidenhead hung but by a thread, and fearing that my opponent would sooner or later betray me, I unbuttoned my jerkin and revealed to the Captain my firm white breasts. 'Look, sir,' I said, 'and behold a virgin who disguised herself at Bragoditz so as to preserve her honour from the soldiery, and who, since God and her good fortune have entrusted her to your care, hopes and prays that you, as an honourable cavalier, will continue to protect it.' And with that I began to weep so bitterly that I could have sworn I really meant it.

The Captain, though quite dumbfounded, could not help laughing at the new name I had invented for my special and private parts. He consoled me with great kindness and promised most fervently to protect my honour. But by his actions he showed that in fact he intended to be the first to go after my maidenhead, and his shameless scrabblings pleased me far better than his honourable protestations. Yet I defended myself bravely, not, indeed, to escape him and his lust, but rather to inflame his passion the more, in which I succeeded so well that I allowed him no favour until he had promised me by all that was holy that he would marry me—though I might have known that he would no more think of keeping his promise than of breaking his neck on purpose. So much, then, for you, my fine Simplex, who thought in Griesbach, perhaps, that you were the first to skim the sweet cream off the milk. Far from it, you poor, deluded fool! It was gone long ago—before you were born, perhaps—and so, having bestirred yourself too late, you got nothing of it but the dregs. Yet all this is mere child's play compared with what else I did to mock you and lead you by the nose, which you shall hear all in its proper time and place.

Chapter Four

s o now I lived with my Captain in secret love and served him both as page and wife. I frequently entreated him to keep his promise and take me to church, but always he had some excuse for postponing this formality. Nothing vexed him more than my habit of abandoning myself most passionately to his caresses while simultaneously lamenting, like Jephtha's daughter, the loss of my maidenhood—though in truth I would not have given a groat for it. On the contrary, I was glad to be rid of its vexatious and wellnigh insufferable yoke, for now at least my wanton urges were assuaged. However, my endearments and importunings at least prevailed upon him to the extent of having a splendid dress made for me in Vienna, after the latest fashion as worn by the fine ladies of Italy in those days. So now I lacked nothing but the married state and the title of a Captain's wife. With this gift he greatly raised my hopes and kept me compliant, though I was never permitted to wear the dress or, indeed, display myself in any way as a woman, far less as his consort. But what vexed me most was that he no longer called me Janco, nor yet Libuschka, but Courage. Others began to use the name as well, without knowing whence it came, thinking merely that my master called me thus for the splendid and matchless gallantry I invariably displayed in the face of the enemy. And so I was compelled to suffer it, albeit with a bad grace. Therefore, ye young maidens who have kept your honour and your maidenhood still unsullied, be warned and do not take its loss lightly, for with it goes your freedom, which you exchange for the thraldom of temptations so imperious and tormenting that they are harder to bear than death itself. I have experienced them in my own flesh and can tell a tale of them.

So, though the loss of my maidenhead did not trouble me—never having felt any urge to put it under lock and key—I was greatly vexed by the mockery I had to endure into the bargain. Indeed, I was compelled even to put a good face on it, for fear that my Captain should let the cat out of the bag and expose me to public shame and derision. And so you, too, ye bucks and gallants who practise such base deception, beware that your trifling does not receive its just reward at the hands of those whose vengeance you thus provoke. Remember the cavalier in Paris who, after deceiving a lady and announcing his intention of wedding another, was enticed back to his lover's bed and there murdered at dead of night, cruelly mutilated and thrown out of the window into the street. As for me, I may as well confess that had my Captain not been so adept at satisfying my urges with his attentions, and at keeping alive the hope that surely he would yet marry me one day, I would, on some suitable occasion, have put a bullet through his head.

Meanwhile we marched under General Bucquoy's command into Hungary, where we began by occupying Pressburg. We left most of our baggage and treasure there, for my Captain foresaw that we would have to face a pitched battle with Bethlen Gabor. Thence we moved on to St Georgi, Poessing, Moder and other places, which we first looted and then burned to the ground. We occupied Tirnau, Altenburg and almost the whole of the island, but before Neusoll we received some hard knocks. Not only was my Captain mortally wounded, but General Bucquoy himself was killed in this battle, and his death made us take to our heels and not stop until we were back in Pressburg.

There I nursed my Captain most devotedly, but the surgeons told him that there was no hope of saving his life because his lung was injured. Devout friends encouraged and admonished him to make his peace with God, and our regimental chaplain was so diligent a saviour of souls that he gave him no rest until he had been shriven and received the last communion. This done, he was spurred and driven, by his confessor as much as by his conscience, to give me his hand in marriage on his sickbed—for the benefit of his soul rather than the pleasures of the flesh. And this he did the more readily since I had persuaded him that I was with child by him. Such is the mad way of the world: others take wives so as to live with them in wedlock, but this one married me because he knew that he was dying! From these events it became public knowledge that I had served him not so much as a faithful servant but as his mistress, and that I had the greater cause to grieve at his fate. The splendid dress he had given me now served its purpose nobly for the wedding ceremony, though my pleasure in it was short-lived, since a few days afterwards he died and left me a widow, in which capacity I had to exchange it for a black one. Then could I truthfully echo the woman who replied to her friend's condolences at her husband's funeral: 'Love a thing well enough and you may be sure it will be the first that the Devil will take from you.' I gave him as splendid a funeral as his rank and station merited, for he had left me not only some fine horses, weapons and clothes, but also a goodly sum of money. And of all these events I made the scribes give me a written statement, in the hope that it might serve me to lay my hands on some of his parents' estate as well. But search as I might I could discover no more about him than that he was, indeed, of noble birth, though so impoverished that his plight would have been parlous indeed had the Bohemians not come to his rescue with a war.

Not only did I lose my lover in Pressburg, but I was also besieged there for a time by Bethlen Gabor. But when ten companies of horse and two regiments of foot from Moravia relieved the city by dint of a feint or stratagem, Bethlen despaired of taking it and raised the siege. So I availed myself of a suitable opportunity to move with my horses, servants and baggage to Vienna, in the hope of returning thence to Bohemia and seeing whether my nurse in Bragoditz was still alive and could at last tell me who my parents were. For it gave me great pleasure in those days to imagine with what honour and respect I would be received in my home town with so many horses and servants—all, as the scribe's statement testified, honestly acquired in war.

Chapter Five

I DISCOVERED that I would have to wait a while before setting out on my intended journey from Vienna to Bragoditz, for the roads were quite unsafe and the inns along the way fleeced travellers unmercifully. So I sold my horses, dismissed all my servants, hiring a maid instead, and took lodgings consisting of a room, a chamber and a kitchen in a widow's house, so as to manage circumspectly until I might find an opportunity which would see me safely home. This widow was as ripe a slut as you would find in a month's travels. Her two daughters resembled us in that they, too, were whores, and both well known to the striplings at court and the officers of the garrison. It was not long before they had spread word among these coxcombs concerning the grace and beauty of the Captain's widow who lodged with them. But I, as befitted my widow's weeds, which set me apart and lent me an air of grave sobriety as well as providing a striking setting for my fair complexion, began by leading a quiet and withdrawn life. I set my maid to spin, and busied myself with sewing, weaving and other work appropriate to my sex, letting who would observe me at it. But secretly I preened myself for my beauty and would stand in front of the mirror by the hour, learning and practising how to laugh, weep, sigh and otherwise alter my countenance to my best advantage. This folly was proof enough of my wantonness, and a clear indication that I would soon follow in the footsteps of my hostess' daughters. They, for their part, hastened to make my better acquaintance, calling on me in my rooms to pass the time of day with such conversation as would be least likely to preserve a young creature like me in the ways of piety and chastity, especially one with my powerful natural urges. With many a merry joke and pretty compliment they began by instructing my maid how to dress and adorn me according to the latest fashion, and me they taught how to make my fair skin even whiter and my golden hair glossier. And when they had tricked me out they exclaimed what a pity it was that so lovely a creature should still be condemned to black robes and the life of a turtle dove. This was sweet music to my ears and rich fuel further to inflame my passions. They also lent me books of chivalry to while away the hours and to learn from them compliments and fine turns of speech. In short, they left nothing undone that in their view could tempt me to amorous adventures.

Meanwhile the servants whom I had dismissed had spread abroad what kind of a Captain's wife I had been and how I had come by this title. And as they did not know how else to call me, the name of Courage stuck to me. As for me, the memory of my Captain began to fade since he served no longer to keep me warm and satisfied, and the reports that I had of the pleasure and profit which my hostess' daughters derived from their adventures made my mouth water for similar fare. My hostess would gladly and selflessly have been the first to provide me with what I lacked, but while I was still in mourning she dared not broach the subject openly and to my face, for she perceived that I haughtily rejected any proposals of this kind. Nevertheless there were several men of good breeding who importuned her daily on my behalf and who swarmed around the house like robber bees around the honey pot. Among them was a young Count who had seen me in church of late and incontinently fallen in love with me. This youth paid her well to make my acquaintance, but despite all his pleadings she dared not make so bold as to introduce him to my rooms. The Count therefore sought out some of my former servants and questioned them closely about the regiment in which my Captain had served. When he had made himself familiar with the names of the officers he called on me to pay his humble respects and to inquire after these his 'acquaintances', whom he had never seen in his life. This carried him on to my Captain, of whom he boasted that in their youth they had shared a bench at their studies and had always been the best of friends and companions. He lamented his untimely death, pitied me in my bereavement at so tender an age and offered me whatever help it was in his power to give and in my discretion to accept, and so on and so forth. With these and similar expressions of sympathy and concern the young spark tried to pay me his court, and though I knew he was lying (for my husband had never studied in his life) I accepted his remarks with a good grace, for it was easy to see that he intended to take my Captain's place with me. Yet I showed myself cold and distant, answered him but briefly, and even forced a few becoming tears. I thanked him for his kind words and offers of help with such turns of phrase as would make him realise that on his first visit he must needs rest content with a good beginning and honourably take his leave.

The next day he sent his servant to inquire whether it would inconvenience me if he called on me again. I replied that though it would cause me no inconvenience and I was, indeed, very ready to receive him, the world was full of wrong-headed people to whom everything was a cause for suspicion, wherefore I begged him to spare me and not bring me into evil repute.

This cold reply, far from angering the Count, only increased his ardour. He passed by the house with a melancholy air, hoping at least to feast his eyes with a glimpse of me at the window, but in vain. I intended to sell my wares as dearly as I could and hid myself from view.

Now while the Count was languishing for unrequited love, I put my mourning aside and dressed myself in my other gown. I also used every trick I knew to enhance my beauty still more, and so drew upon me the eyes and hearts of many men of rank and station. But this happened only when I went to church, for otherwise I never left the house. I began to receive many tokens and messages every day from men who suffered from the same sickness as my Count, but I stood as firm as a rock, until all Vienna was abuzz not only with my incomparable beauty but also with the fame of my chastity and other rare virtues. When matters had reached the point where I was almost taken for a saint, I decided that the time had come for me to give free rein to those impulses of the flesh which hitherto I had so firmly kept in check, and simultaneously to confound all those who held so high an opinion of me.

The Count was the first on whom I bestowed my favours, seeing that he had spared neither effort nor expense to obtain them. Moreover, since I found him to my taste and he loved me to distraction, I concluded that of all that rabble he was the most likely to satisfy my needs. Yet even so he would not have prevailed had he not presented me, when first I came out of mourning, with a length of fine Brussels lace, as well as the cloth and trimmings for a handsome new dress and, above all, with one hundred ducats for my household—to help console me the better, as he said, for the loss of my husband. The next to follow him was the ambassador of a great potentate, who gave me sixty ducats for my first night's pay. After him there were others, but only such as were ready to spend lavishly. As for the poor, or rather the less rich and well situated, they might cool their heels outside the door or make do with my hostess' daughters. In the event I so managed my affairs that my mills, so to speak, never stood idle, and I ground away to such purpose that within a month I had amassed one thousand ducats in specie, not to mention what I received in jewels, rings, chains, bracelets, velvets, silks, linen (and let none come to me with mere trifles such as gloves or stockings!), victuals, wine and other

43

presents. All this confirmed me in my determination to use my tender years to the full, for I well knew the saying:

> However beautiful you be
> The years will take it all from thee.

And, indeed, I would regret it to this day had I done less. In the end my way of life became so notorious that people began to point their fingers at me and I could calculate with certainty that matters were bound to end badly, for by this time I was accepting even lesser fry. My hostess was my faithful helpmeet, much to her own profit. She taught me all manner of tricks, known not only to wantons but also to those who follow in the train of loose-living men, even to the point of making myself impregnable and capable of blocking a man's musket so that it would not fire. I do believe that had I stayed with her longer I would even have learned the art of witchcraft.

But when I had been given fair warning that the city fathers intended to clean out our nest and destroy it, I bought myself a coach and two horses, hired a servant and suddenly departed, for just at that time a good opportunity offered to get me safely home.

Chapter Six

IN Prague I had every opportunity to continue the pursuit of my trade, but the desire to see my nurse again and to discover who were my parents spurred me on to Bragoditz. With the country-side once more at peace, I had every reason to expect a safe journey, but as ill luck would have it, one evening when I could already see my destination from afar, eleven of Mansfeld's troopers appeared, whom I took, as anyone else would have done, for Imperial troops and good friends, for they wore red sashes and the Imperial arms. They seized me and set off with me and my coach towards the Bohemian Forest as if the Devil himself had been at their heels. I screamed to make the welkin ring, but they quickly silenced me, and about midnight arrived at a lonely inn at the edge of the Forest. There they supped, and then they dealt with me as soldiers are accustomed to do with lonely and defenceless women. Though this troubled me far less than the loss of my coach and possessions, it turned out as badly for them as dry land does for a fish. For while they were having their lewd will with me, a Captain and thirty dragoons who had been escorting a convoy to Pilsen surprised and seized them, and since, by the false favours they wore, they had

45

forfeited the right to be regarded as prisoners of war, they were all put to the sword. My captors had not yet shared out my treasures among them, and since I was in possession of an Imperial pass and had been a captive for less than twenty-four hours, I pointed out to the Captain that he could not regard and seize me and my belongings as rightful booty. This he was compelled to admit, but maintained that I was nevertheless obliged to him for my deliverance and could not take it amiss if he refused to relinquish this prize which he had won in a fair fight. If, as my pass proclaimed, I was a Captain's widow, he, for his part, was a widowed Captain. If I were willing, the question of the spoils could be settled quickly enough; if not, he would take me with him notwithstanding and argue later about his rights with any who might wish to challenge them. From this I rightly surmised that he had already taken a fancy to me, and to press the point further in his favour he added that he would leave me to choose whether the booty should be divided among all his men equally, or whether I preferred to commend myself and my treasure to his personal care by marrying him. If I agreed to this offer he would undertake to persuade his men that I was not a legitimate prize but must join him in wedlock unscathed and undiminished. I replied that if the choice were mine indeed, I would ask for neither, but rather that he should let me continue my journey safely under his protection, and with that I began to weep bitterly, as if I had been in deadly earnest, according to the rhyme:

> See now how women often weep,
> Though the hurt is not so deep.
> Shrewdest of deceivers still
> They shed bitter tears at will.
> He who heeds their loud lament
> On fool's errand oft is bent,
> For their slyly practised wiles
> Are falser than the Crocodile's.
> Let her sob and let her moan,
> Wring her fingers to the bone,

Do not trust her, but be wise,
For her sorrow is but lies.
She says nay with many an oath
Yet in her heart she is not loth
And would rather be foresworn
Than have her dress and bodice torn.
'No' most commonly means 'Yes',
If you do your suit but press,
And your caresses, close and kind,
Will quickly make her change her mind.

Exactly after this manner did I comport myself, thinking thereby to give him occasion to console me and so to fan his passion.
For I knew well enough that the proud hearts of men are most
easily moved by weeping and sorrowing women. My ruse succeeded as well as I could have wished. He raised me up and
spoke kindly to me, assuring me of his love with many protestations. In the end I gave my consent, but with the strict condition and reservation that he should not lay hands on me before
our marriage, to which he agreed and scrupulously kept his
word until we came to the former Mansfeld fortress of Waid-
hausen which the General had recently yielded to the Duke of
Bavaria under a settlement. There my lover, whose passion,
now thoroughly aroused, would brook no further delay to our
wedding night, took my hand in marriage before ever he had
had a chance to discover by what trade Courage had earned her
handsome dowry. I had hardly been with the regiment a
month before I encountered several officers who had not only
known me in Vienna, but had been good customers of mine
into the bargain. Though they were discreet and well mannered
enough not to make a public scandal of my shame and their
own, yet I could not prevent some talk. But it troubled me little,
except that I was once again afflicted with the nickname of
Courage.

For the rest, I had a good, patient husband who was as pleased
with my gold as he was with my charms. The latter, it is true, he
used more sparingly than I could have wished, but to make up

for it permitted me all the more freedom in my speech and behaviour towards others. Whenever this led his companions to tease him with warnings of an impending growth of horns, he would answer good-humouredly that it was of no great concern to him. If anyone should, indeed, happen to bestride his wife he would not leave matters there but would take care to alter and improve upon his work. He always kept an excellent horse for me, richly caparizoned, which I was accustomed to ride, not with a side saddle like other officers' wives, but astride. If by chance I did use a side saddle I would always carry a pair of pistols and a Turkish sabre under my thigh and have a stirrup ready on the other side. As I also wore breeches under my thin taffeta skirt I could at any moment resume my position astride and be taken for a young trooper. Whenever we had a brush with the enemy I found it more than I could bear to stand aside and take no part. It was, on the contrary, my frequent contention that a lady who dared not defend herself against a man on horseback had no right to wear gay plumes like a man. In some small skirmishes I even succeeded in taking a prisoner or two who thought themselves no cowards, and from then on ventured to arm myself for such encounters with a carbine or a flintlock, and even to take on two opponents at a time. And this I did the more readily since by virtue of the art I had learned from my hostess I had made myself and my horse so hard that no bullet could pierce us.

That is how I fared in those days, and made for myself more booty than many a regular soldier, which was bound to offend a good many of them. But since it buttered my bread I took no notice of their grumbles. My husband let me do exactly as I wished, and the trust he reposed in me kept me faithful to him, incapable though he was of satisfying my natural appetites. But I was as merry in company and as forward and bold in conversation as I was brave in the face of the enemy, and withal thrifty and houseproud as any woman in the field, better than a good equerry in the care of horses, and in camp so well heeled that my husband could have wished for no better wife.

Even when he had reason—as sometimes happened—to object to what I did, he would not take it amiss if I contradicted him and carried on in my own sweet way, for as a result our wealth increased so greatly that we found ourselves obliged to pass on a good part of it for safe keeping to merchants in one of the larger towns. In this way I lived happily and prosperously, and would never have asked for a better fate—if only my husband had been somewhat better mounted!

But my stars, or the goddess of Fortune, did not suffer me long to enjoy this happy state, for my husband was shot dead at Wisloch and so, after a brief term of marriage, I found myself a widow once more.

Chapter Seven

MY husband was scarcely cold and buried before I found myself with a round dozen of new suitors and the need to choose between them. For I was endowed not only with youth and beauty, but also with fine horses and a respectable fortune. So, although I let it be known that I would spend six months in mourning for my dear departed Captain, I could not escape the importunate throng that swarmed around me like bumblebees round a honey jar with a broken lid. The Colonel allowed me board and lodgings with the regiment until I could make other arrangements, and I appointed two servants to do the man's work in the household. I myself continued as reckless of my safety as any soldier whenever I thought there was a chance of a prize. At the gay and diverting encounter of Wimpfen, for instance, I captured a Lieutenant, and in the pursuit that followed the skirmish an Ensign with his standard. As for my two servants, they plundered the wagons and made a good haul of ready money, of which I got my share according to our agreement.

After this encounter I found myself with even more suitors than before. As I had enjoyed the days better than the nights with my last husband and had, since his death, been reduced to a total and irksome abstinence, I was determined to ensure that my next choice should compensate me for any past privations. I therefore became betrothed to a Lieutenant who in my eyes excelled all his rivals in looks, youth, wit and vigour. He was Italian by birth, with black hair and a white skin, and I thought him so handsome that no artist could have painted him better. Until he had subjected me to his spell he treated me with well-nigh dog-like devotion, and when at last I plighted him my troth he fell into such transports of delight as if he had been given the whole world as a birthday present. We were married in the Palatinate and honoured at the wedding by the presence of the Colonel and most of the other senior officers, who wished us, though in vain, much happiness and many years of married bliss.

But as we lay idly abed together at dawn after the first night, exchanging caresses and words of endearment before rising, my Lieutenant summoned his page to his bedside and ordered him to fetch two stout cudgels. The lad did as he was told and I, imagining that the poor devil would be the first to have a taste of them, hastened to plead for him in his absence. He returned, laid the cudgels on the table beside the ewer as he was bidden and withdrew. Then my bridegroom said to me: 'Now, my love, you know how it was common gossip and report in the regiment that during your previous marriage you wore the breeches, which brought your late husband into some contempt among sensible folk. This gives me reason to fear that you may wish to persist in your habit and wear mine as well, which I could never suffer—or at least not willingly. I have therefore, as you see, had these two staves laid on the table so that, should you still wish to claim the breeches and maintain your possession of them as before, we may first fight for them. You must admit it is better that their fate should be decided here and now, rather than that we should fight for them daily throughout our married life.'

Giving him a most affectionate kiss I replied: 'I fancied, my own Dearest, that the joust in which we intended to engage had already been fought out this night, and had no thought of aspiring to your breeches. Far from it, for I know that Woman was taken from Man's side, not from his head. I had hoped that this would be known to you also, and that you, remembering whence I came, would treat me as your consort rather than your door-mat, seeing that I have not been taken from the soles of your feet. I was the more secure in this expectation since I did not presume to sit on your head but am well content to lie by your side. Wherefore I beg you most humbly to abandon all thought of so strange and unseemly a duel.'

'Ho, ho!' he said, 'I can see that you do not lack a woman's wiles, who can make herself mistress of the household even before the husband becomes aware of it. But I, for my part, insist that we should first fight for the breeches, so that I shall know who henceforth owes obedience to the other.' And with that the dolt tore himself from my embraces. So I leaped out of bed, donned my nightshift and drawers, and snatched the shorter but stouter of the two cudgels from the table, saying: 'Since you command me to fight and are ready to let the victor lord it over the vanquished (which I had never contemplated) I would be a fool to decline the chance of winning what otherwise I would never have claimed.'—Seeing me standing there, ready and waiting for him, he eagerly pulled on his breeches, grasped the other cudgel and made as if to seize me by the hair so as to belabour my back at his leisure. But I was much too quick for him, and before he knew where he was struck him such a blow on the head that he staggered dizzily like a stricken ox. I gathered up the two cudgels to throw them out of the door, but when I opened it, several officers stood revealed who had been listening to our argument and seen part of it through a chink. Leaving them to their merriment I slammed the door in their faces, wrapped my skirt around me and revived my booby of a bridegroom with water from the ewer. When I had set him down at the table and somewhat ordered my appearance I admitted the officers to the room to join us.

I leave it to my gentle readers to imagine with what looks we favoured each other. It was clear to me that my bridegroom had invited these his comrades to gather at our door at this hour to witness his folly, for when they had teased him with the danger of my wearing the breeches he had boasted that he knew a fine and effective method, which he would employ the very first morning, of making me so compliant that ever afterwards I would tremble if he so much as gave me a surly look. But the poor clown would have done better to have tried out his method on someone other than Courage. For against her he succeeded merely in making himself a public laughing-stock, nor would I have continued to live with him had not the holy sacrament of marriage ordained it and compelled me to do so. As to the manner of our cohabitation, it can readily be imagined: like cat and dog. At last, seeing no hope of getting his revenge and unable to stomach the regiment's mockery any longer, he gathered together all my money one fine day, and with my three best horses and one of my servants deserted to the enemy.

Chapter Eight

THUS I became a widow-by-halves—an estate much more miserable than being altogether without a husband. Some suspected me of intending to follow him, and that we had planned this our flight jointly. But when I asked the Colonel for his advice and counsel as to what I should do, he told me to stay with the regiment, and if I bore myself honestly he would see to it that I was furnished with all I required like any other widow. In this way I silenced the aforementioned suspicions, but as I had lost my treasure as well as my fine horses, with whose help I had so often carried off rich prizes, I was compelled to live somewhat frugally. Yet I did what I could to mask my poverty and keep up appearances. I still had my two servants to do the man's work, as well as a stable-lad and some indifferent nags or baggage-horses. Of my belongings, and especially of my male attire, I turned what I could into ready money and bought myself a good horse from the proceeds, so that I was once again well mounted. Though I was debarred, as a woman, from riding out on patrols, I had no equal among the foragers. I often longed for another such battle as that of Wimpfen, but these were vain and idle day-dreams. I could but bide my time, for clearly no one would arrange a battle to do me a favour, however much I might desire it. Yet in the meantime I was short of ready money, which was not commonly to be found on foraging expeditions, and so I took to obliging with my person anyone who was willing to pay for it. This gave me both the satisfaction of revenge upon my faithless and runaway husband, and a fair living for myself. I was even able to hire a third servant, a strong and resourceful lad whose duty it was to help me steal while the other two stood guard. This was the life I led until we chased the Duke of Brunswick across the river Main and drowned many of his men in its waters. In this encounter I took my place among the soldiers, and under my Colonel's eye acquitted myself so well that he would not have believed a man capable of such valour, much less a woman. In one of the enemy's counter-charges I captured a Major from under the very noses of his retinue, and when one of them, trying to rescue him, discharged a pistol so close to my head that it knocked off my hat and plumes, I dealt him such a shrewd and clean blow with my sabre that the fellow continued to ride beside me for several paces without his head—a sight both strange and revolting to behold. When the enemy squadron had been dispersed and routed and the Major had given me a fine collection of gold coins, a gold chain and a valuable ring in exchange for his life, I made my lad change horses with him and sent him back to our lines for safe keeping. Then I continued down to the broken bridge where the enemy were drowning wretchedly in the water or being cut down mercilessly on land. While the battle was still raging and all troops close to their colours with no thought of scattering for loot, I seized a coach with six fine bays. Though it contained neither occupants nor money, I found two chests in it full of costly clothes and fine linen.

This, with my lad's help, I also secured and took back to where I had left the Major, who was eating his very heart out with shame at having been captured by a young woman. But when he saw that I carried pistols both in my belt and in my saddle holsters—which, with my carbine, I now proceeded to clean and re-load—and also heard of my previous exploits at Wimpfen, his chagrin abated somewhat and he said the Devil himself might think twice before having anything to do with such a witch. As for me, I went back with my lad (whom I had made as impregnable as myself and my horse) to find some more booty, but on the way encountered the Lieutenant-Colonel of the regiment lying under his horse, who recognized me and called out to me for help. I lifted him on my lad's horse and led him back to our lines where I made him comfortable in my newly acquired coach, keeping the Major company. It passes belief how loudly my praises were sung after this battle, both by my friends and by those who envied me. All were agreed that I was the very Devil incarnate, and at that moment I had no dearer wish than to have been born a man rather than a woman. But these thoughts were as idle as they were foolish, since fate had made me what I was.

It had often occurred to me to pretend to be a hermaphrodite, hoping that in this way I might be allowed to wear breeches publicly and be regarded as a young lad. But alas, my passions had seduced me into giving so many men incontrovertible proof of my true nature that I lacked the stomach to venture on such a pretence. There were too many witnesses who could have contested my claim, and the upshot of it would have been an examination by surgeons and midwives, which would have brought the truth to light. So I managed as best I could, and to any who presumed to censure my unwomanly exploits I used to retort that in times gone by there had also been Amazons who had fought as bravely as men.

To gain the Colonel's favour and to assure myself of his protection against those who envied me my good fortune, I presented him with both the prisoner and the coach and horses, for which he was pleased to give me 200 rixdollars. This sum, together with what I had seized in the fighting and earned by other means already known to the reader, I deposited, as before, in a sizeable town for safe keeping.

While our army, after taking Mannheim, invested Franckenthal and subdued the Palatinate, that of Cordoba and the Prince of Anhalt inflicted another defeat on the Duke of Brunswick and Mansfeld at Fleurus, and in this encounter my run-away husband, the Lieutenant, chanced to be captured, recognized by our men and hanged by his most gallant neck from a tree as a traitor and a deserter. This, though it relieved me of my husband and restored me to the state of widowhood, also made me such a host of enemies who claimed that 'the witch had brought about the poor devil's death by sorcery', that I would gladly have seen him live somewhat longer and suffered him as a husband until he could have bitten the dust elsewhere and come by an honest death, if only it had been written in his stars.

Chapter Nine

BUT as it was, I fell into an even greater disrepute, which grew worse from day to day. My enemies even seduced my servants from their allegiance, upbraiding them and saying: 'Fie on you, that you persist in serving such a jade!' I had hoped to find myself another husband, but men now shook their heads and said to one another: 'You take her, for I would not care to touch her.' Honest folk shunned my company, and so did most of the officers. As for lowlier and less reputable suitors, I would have nothing to do with them and kept them at arm's length. Though I did not have to pay for our foolish quarrel with my neck, as my husband had, yet it afflicted me longer than him his hanging. Gladly would I have sloughed off my skin and slipped into another, but neither my ingrained habits nor the bad company I kept would allow me to change my spots, for I discovered, as do most people, that war made me evil rather than good. Though I decked myself out again in all my finery and laid all manner of snares and bait to trap and beguile the men of my acquaintance,

58

it was all in vain. My name had become a by-word and Courage was notorious throughout the army. Wherever I rode through the lines a thousand voices openly proclaimed my shame so that at last, like a night-owl, I hardly dared venture abroad in daylight. On the march, honest women scorned me, the baggage-train rabble vexed and mocked me, and those unmarried officers who might have protected me in return for a night's favours had to stay close to their regiments, where their scandalous gossip made my name stink even more. All in all, I could see plainly that my affairs were past mending. Though I still had some friends among the officers, most of them had an eye to their own advantage rather than mine, coveting either my money or my fine horse. They served but to offend me with their importuning, nor was there a single one among them who would have married me, either for shame or because they suspected some malign influence that proved a bane to all my husbands, or because they feared me for some other reason that I knew not of.

Therefore I made up my mind to quit the regiment, the army and, indeed, the very war itself. This was the more easily accomplished since the senior officers would long ere this have been glad to see the last of me. Nor do I suppose that there were many honest folk who shed bitter tears at my departure except, perhaps, for a few unmarried blades among the officers of lower rank, for whom I had washed a pair of night-drawers once in a while. The Colonel was tired of having to admit that his fine coach had been captured and presented to him by Courage. The Lieutenant-Colonel whom I had rescued wounded from the battlefield thought it such a disgrace that he would gladly have thanked me for my trouble with an oath, and frowned and blushed so furiously every time he caught sight of me that I could easily imagine what blessings and endearments he left unsaid. The women, and in particular the officers' wives, hated me because I was more beautiful than any of them, and moreover pleased some of their husbands better. Even the soldiers, both high and low, disliked me, for I put them out of countenance by the recklessness and daring with which I attempted and achieved feats the very thought of which made many of them quake in their boots.

Knowing that I had more enemies than friends I did not doubt that sooner or later one of them would, in his or her own dastardly way, seize the chance of doing me an ill turn. 'Ah, Courage,' I said to myself, 'how can you hope to escape such a multitude of foes, each of whom doubtless has his own particular designs upon you? Even if you had naught else than your fine horses, rich dresses, good weapons and the reputation of a well-filled purse, it would be enough for some of them to hire a cut-throat or two to do away with you secretly. How if they did, or if some villain struck you down from behind in an encounter with the enemy? What cock would crow for you? Who would avenge your death? Can you, indeed, trust even your own servants?' With such thoughts I tormented myself, and since I had no steadfast friend to share them must needs keep my own counsel about them and rely only on myself.

In the end I asked the Colonel for a pass to the nearest town that took my fancy and seemed to offer a suitable retreat from warfare. I obtained it readily enough, and for good measure and in lieu of discharge a document certifying that I had been properly married to a Captain of the regiment (for of my last husband I desired no references), had dwelt for a time after his death with the regiment and had there comported myself piously and soberly as befitted a chaste, virtuous and honourable lady whose righteous and unblemished conduct would commend her to all whom this document might concern. These outrageous and flagrant lies the Colonel formally endorsed with his own signature and seal. Nor need anyone marvel at this, for the worse a person's conduct has been and the greater the desire to be rid of him, the more fervent will be the adieus with which he is sent on his way, especially if they must also serve in lieu of payment. I for my part, and as a token of my gratitude, made the Colonel a present of a servant and a horse—the latter fit for an officer—and took with me only one servant, a stable lad, a maid, six fine horses (one of them worth a hundred ducats at least) and a well-furnished wagon; and by my faith (or should I say my perfidy?) I cannot tell how I came to possess all these goods and chattels—though my readers will doubtless hazard a guess.

When I and my suite had safely reached the aforementioned town I turned my horses into silver and sold whatever else would fetch money and which I did not particularly need. For thrift's sake I also dismissed all my servants. But as in Vienna, so here, too, I discovered that I could not rid myself of the name Courage, which of all my possessions was the one I would have sold most cheaply. For my young army clients came riding into town after me and asked for me by that name, which the children in the alleys learned more quickly than the Lord's prayer. This vexed me so much that I showed these young gallants the door, but they were not slow to take their revenge, telling the townsfolk such things about me as I would gladly have kept hidden. However, with the help of the Colonel's letter and seal I proved the contrary, and persuaded my neighbours that the young officers spread such wicked tales about me for no better reason than that I would not gratify their lewd desires. In this way I established a fair reputation for myself, and with the aid of my good written report and in return for a small payment prevailed upon the town to take me under its protection until such time as I could make other arrangements. And so, much against my inclinations, I conducted myself there most honourably, piously, quietly and modestly, carefully tending my good looks, which seemed to improve with the years, in the hope of sooner or later finding myself yet another vigorous and ardent husband.

Chapter Ten

BUT I could have waited a long time before I landed a good catch, for persons of breeding made their choice among their own kind, and other men of wealth had no trouble in finding rich, beautiful, and above all virtuous damsels to marry (something to which in those days some value still attached), rather than burdening themselves with a cast-off soldiers' whore. On the other hand there were some who had either been made bankrupt or were in imminent danger of it, and these, it is true, would willingly have married me for my money; but for that very reason I would have none of them. As for artisans and traders, they were beneath my dignity, and so I remained single for a whole year, which was quite contrary to my nature and almost more than I could bear, especially as the good life I led was making me exceedingly lecherous. This good life I owed to the money I had salted away from time to time in different towns and cities, entrusting it to merchants and usurers. It afforded me so ample an income that I could live much at my ease without ever touching the principal. It was not here, in fact, that the shoe pinched me, but rather between my thighs, which either would not or could not endure this lush but solitary life any longer. So I sent my money to Prague by letter of credit and set out there myself somewhat later in the company of a group of merchants, to seek refuge with my nurse in Bragoditz and see if perchance better luck might attend me there.

I found her much reduced in fortune since my departure, for not only had the war pressed her hard, but even before that she had lived more at my expense than I at her's. She was overjoyed to see me, especially when she realized that I had not come empty-handed. Her first welcome, nevertheless, was exceedingly tearful, and even as she kissed me she called me a miserable young gentlewoman who would be hard put to it to lead a life befitting her rank and descent. No longer, she continued, would she be able to help, advise and guide me as she had done in times gone by, for my best friends and relations had all been either exiled or killed. Moreover, she said, if the Emperor's supporters were ever to discover my origin and pedigree I durst scarcely show my face among them. All this she uttered amidst copious sobs, so that I could barely hear, much less understand, what she was saying and could make neither head nor tail of it. But when I had calmed her and regaled her with food and drink until her cheeks began to glow red (for the poor old crone was living on the shortest of commons) she told me very frankly about my origins, saying that my natural father had been a Count, and until a few years ago the most powerful in the whole kingdom, but now, on account of his rebellion against the Emperor, banished from the country. The latest tidings of him were that he was at the Turkish Porte, where he was even said to have exchanged his Christian religion for that of the Turks. As for my mother, she said she had been gently bred, but as poor as she was beautiful. She had been a lady of the Countess' bedchamber, and while she waited upon the Countess, the Count, for his part, waited upon her in her own bedchamber to such purpose that in the end he had to send her to the castle of a nobleman of his acquaintance where she was delivered of me. My nurse happened to be at this castle at the same time, just having given birth to a son whom the nobleman had fathered on her, and so she became my wet-nurse and later my guardian and retainer in Bragoditz, where both my father and my mother had supplied her with sufficient means for my upkeep. 'Your father had promised you in marriage,' she concluded, 'to a gallant young nobleman, but the Imperial troops captured him when they took Pilsen and hanged him, together with several others, as a traitor.'

In this manner I discovered what I had long wanted to know, yet now I would gladly have remained in ignorance of it, seeing what little profit my distinguished birth would most probably bring me. I took counsel with myself what best to do in the circumstances, and in the end made an arrangement with my former wet-nurse that henceforth she should be my mother and I her daughter. She was far more cunning than I, and so I accepted her advice that we should leave Bragoditz and move to Prague, both to escape the scrutiny of those who might know us of old, and in the hope of encountering better fortune there.

For the rest, we were well suited to each other. Not, I mean, that she should go pandering and I whoring, but because she was in need of a provider and I of a faithful retainer such as her, to whom I could entrust my honour and my wealth. For even without counting my clothes and trinkets I owned at that time some 3,000 rixdollars in cash, and consequently had no need to seek a shameful living.

I dressed my new mother like an honourable old matron, paid her every respect, and in public showed her the greatest deference. We gave ourselves out to be two unfortunate gentlewomen driven out of Germany by the war, and earned a living by sewing and fine needlework in silk and gold and silver thread. We lived, indeed, very quietly and secluded, carefully nursing our pennies which, for lack of such care, have a habit of melting away unawares and are then not easily replaced when most needed. This life we led would have been a fine and wellnigh saintly one, had we but had the resolution to persist in it. But I soon found myself beset once more by admirers. Some sought me as men do a woman in a brothel, others, too bashful to offer payment for my honour, were ninnies who prated of marriage, but all were at pains to persuade me that their lust was inspired by a deep and lasting love. Yet there was not one among them whom I would have trusted, even if I had had so much as a drop of chaste blood left in my veins. I was no more than the living proof of the old proverb that deep calls unto deep, for just as they say that you cannot conceal straw in a boot, spindles in a sack or a whore in a house, so I, too, quickly became known for what I was, though also renowned everywhere for my beauty. This brought me much employment for our needles, including an order for a sword sash from a Captain who pretended to be breathing his last for love of me. I, for my part, told him such tall tales of my chastity that he all but believed me and despaired of his conquest. For I judged the quality and fortune of my clients according to the guiding rule of mine host at the Golden Lion in N., who explained it to me thus: 'When a patron treats me with great courtesy and many compliments it is a sure sign that his credit is poor or that for some other reason he is unwilling to spend freely. But if a man comes and thumps the table and shows himself haughty and overbearing, I say to myself "ho, this fellow's purse is well lined and he is ripe for fleecing". So I treat the flatterers with flattery and compliments in order that they may spread abroad my and my hostelry's praises, and the bullies I serve with all they desire, so as to pluck them clean afterwards.'

But while I was treating the Captain as mine host his courteous guests he, for his part, saw in me, if not the better part of an angel, at any rate the very model and image of chastity. To be brief, he reached the point where he began babbling of marriage and would not listen to reason until I had given him my consent. The marriage contract provided that I should make over to him 1,000 rixdollars in cash to deposit in Germany, where he lived, and that the money should revert to me if he died before me without issue. My remaining 2,000 rixdollars I would put to usury in an agreed place, the interest to be consumed by us jointly during our marriage, but the principal to remain untouched until we had children. I was, moreover, to retain the right, if I died without issue, to leave my entire fortune, including the 1,000 rixdollars made over to him, to whomsoever I wished. When this was settled the marriage took place, and just as we were looking forward to seeing the war out in Prague, living comfortably in the garrison as if in peacetime, behold, orders came for us to set out for Holstein and take part in the Danish war.

Chapter Eleven

I EQUIPPED myself very thoroughly for this campaign, knowing far better than the Captain, my husband, what was required for such an enterprise. But fearing that I might once again find myself in company where the name of Courage and her reputation were known, I told my husband all about my past life, omitting only my spells of whoring here and there and how I had lived disguised as a page with my first husband before I married him. As for my name Courage, I persuaded him that I had won it for my fearlessness, as was, indeed, commonly believed by that time. With this account I forestalled those who might otherwise have brought me into ill odour with him by telling him my life's story and adding more, perhaps, than I would have liked him to know. And in this I succeeded, for just as he would not believe me when I told him of my exploits in battle until they were later confirmed by those who had witnessed them, so also he refused to credit those that spoke ill to him of my past, because I roundly denied their tales. For the rest he was a very deliberate, sensible man in his actions, of excellent presence and also fearless and resourceful in battle, so that I often came to wonder why he had married me, for by rights he deserved someone of better repute.

My 'mother', who had no thought of being left behind, came with me as housekeeper and cook, and I provisioned our baggage wagon with everything that could be of the least use to us in the field. I did this so thoroughly and directed the servants to such purpose that my husband never had to trouble himself with it or to charge a steward with its execution. For my own part, I equipped myself once again with a good horse, saddle and bridle, and with a musket, and in such excellent fettle we joined Tilly's army. There I was soon recognized and welcomed with a good deal of chaff and banter. 'Be of good cheer, brothers,' they shouted to one another, 'here is a good omen for victory in battle. And why? Because Courage is with us once more!' Nor did their ribald judgement lack some measure of sound sense, for the force we brought with us consisted of three regiments of horse and two of foot, a reinforcement by no means to be despised and likely to provide the army with enough courage even without my presence.

It was two days, as I remember it, after this auspicious juncture that we came to grips with the King of Denmark's troops at Lutter. Once again, I had no intention of staying with the baggage, and so, when the enemy's first assault was blunted and our own troops closed ranks for the counter-charge, I fought my way into the thick of the battle, intent on carrying off some unusual prize, so as to prove to my husband once and for all that he had made no mean bargain with me of which he need be ashamed. I laid about me with my sabre to ease the way for my noble stallion, which had not its equal in all Prague, until I succeeded in seizing a Captain of horse, of noble Danish blood, by the forelock and dragging him back through the confusion to my baggage wagon. Though my horse and I received some hard knocks we did not leave so much as a drop of blood on the battlefield, sustaining no more than a few bumps and weals. Encouraged by the success of my first sally I reloaded my musket and dashed back into the fray, where this time I seized a Quartermaster and a common trooper, neither of whom was aware that I was a woman until I had taken them to join the Captain of horse where my servants were. I searched none of them, for each surrendered of his own free will what he had on him by way of money or money's worth. And in particular I saw to it that the Captain was treated with courtesy, and did not permit him to be touched, much less stripped. But when I absented myself awhile on purpose, my servants exchanged clothes with the other two, whose garments were adorned with exceptionally fine ruffs and lace. I would have risked a third sally and continued to strike while the iron was hot and the battle raging, but I feared to impose upon my good horse. However, my husband was also awarded some small prizes from those who had retired into the castle of Lutter and there surrendered unconditionally; so that jointly we got, during and after the battle, in all some 1,000 guilders' worth of booty from the enemy, which we sent straightway to Prague by letter of credit, to add to my 2,000 rixdollars already deposited there, for we did not need it in the field and lived in daily hope of even fatter prizes.

My husband and I loved each other better from day to day, and each thought himself blessed to have the other in marriage. Had we not both felt it improper, we would never have left each other's side, day or night, whether on watch, among the earthworks or in battle. We left to each other all we possessed, so that the survivor (whether we had issue or not) would inherit everything from the one to die first, with due provision made for the maintenance of my nurse and foster-mother for her lifetime, for she had shown us great loyalty and rendered us faithful service. This last will and testament we had drawn up in duplicate and deposited one copy with the Senate in Prague and the other in my husband's home town in Germany, which at that time was still flourishing and quite untouched by war.

After the encounter at Lutter we occupied Steinbruck, Verden, Langenwedel, Rothenburg, Ottersburg and the castle of Hoya, where my husband was ordered to remain with an assorted body of troops placed under his command for the purpose, but without their baggage train. And just as I would never let myself be parted from my husband when danger threatened, so now, too, I would not leave him alone in this castle for fear that the lice would eat him up. For there were no women there to help the soldiers to keep clean. But our baggage stayed with the regiment, which marched off to enjoy its winter quarters, where I would gladly have joined them.

As soon as these dispositions had been made at the approach of winter and Tilly had thus dispersed his forces, behold, the King of Denmark returned with his army, intending to recapture during the winter what he had lost in the summer. He invested Verden, but because it proved too hard a nut for him to crack he vented his wrath on the castle of Hoya, bombarding it for seven days with more than a thousand cannon balls, one of which struck my beloved husband and made me, for the fourth time, a most desolate and wretched widow.

Chapter Twelve

AT last our troops, fearful lest the castle should crumble and bury us all under its ruins, surrendered to the King and were allowed to withdraw. But I, marching with them in great sorrow and distress, had the further misfortune to be recognized by the Major whom I had captured in the battle against the Duke of Brunswick on the banks of the Main. He hastened to make inquiries about me, and having assured himself as to my identity and also discovered how I had so recently been bereaved, waited his chance and suddenly snatched me from the ranks of the column. 'You bloody witch,' he said, 'now will I repay you for the shame you brought upon me that day at Hoechst. I will teach you such a lesson that henceforth you will never want to bear arms again or presume to make a prize of a gentleman.' He looked so thunderously fierce that his frown was enough to strike terror in my heart, though had I but been astride my good black stallion I would soon have taught him to keep a civil tongue in his head. However, he drove me before him to a troop of his own horsemen and set an Ensign to guard me, who questioned me about all that had formerly passed between me and the Lieutenant-Colonel (for this was now his rank). Then he told me that the other had nearly forfeited his head, or at least his rank, for having allowed himself to be plucked from the very midst of his retinue by a woman, thereby causing great confusion and disarray among his troops. He had only escaped punishment by swearing that I had bewitched him. Yet in the end his shame forced him to resign his commission and take service with the Danes.

The following night we lodged in poorly furnished quarters, where my Lieutenant-Colonel forced me, in revenge for his shame, as he put it, to satisfy his beastly lust, though (fie upon such folly!) there could be naught of pleasure or contentment in the act. And though I made no great effort to resist him he plied me throughout with blows instead of kisses. The following morning they took to their heels like startled hares with the hounds on their trail, which made me think that Tilly must be chasing them. Yet it was only for fear of being chased, without any evidence of it, that they fled. The second night they found quarters where their host was more amenable and treated them better, so my valiant hero of an officer invited others of his ilk to join him and partake of my favours as well; and so, for once, my commonly insatiable lust was thoroughly quenched. The third night, after they had again spent the day running as if the Devil were after them, I fared no better, but rather worse, if anything. I had but barely survived it, letting all these stallions ram themselves into a stupor upon me (for shame! and it is only with difficulty that I speak of it, but must needs for your sweet sake, my Simplici!) when I was compelled, in the sight of all the officers, to let their servants treat me likewise. Up to this point I had borne all that befell me patiently, thinking that my past misdeeds deserved no better, but when it came to this I was gripped by such horror and revulsion that I began to cry out and curse, and call on God for help and vengeance. But I received no mercy from these brutes, who had abandoned all shame and Christian honour. They stripped me naked and threw a few handfuls of peas on the ground, forcing me to bend down and gather them while they tickled my rump and thighs with hazel switches and even seasoned them with salt and pepper, making me leap and caper like a donkey with a bunch of thorns and thistles tied under his tail. I verily believe that had it not been winter they would even have scourged me with nettles.

Then they discussed whether to deliver me up to the stable lads or to try and hang me as a sorceress. The latter, they considered, would do them little honour since they had already made so free with my body. Moreover, the most discreet among them (if any of these brutes could be said to have so much as a spark of discretion left) maintained that if this had been their intention, then my Lieutenant-Colonel should never have laid hands on me in the first place, but handed me over to justice. So in the end it was decided to hand me over to the stable lads in the afternoon, for on that day they plainly felt more secure and were no longer poised for flight. Now when they had tired of the wretched spectacle of me gathering peas, I was permitted to put on my clothes again, and had barely done so when a cavalier rode up and asked to speak with the Lieutenant-Colonel. It was the very Captain of horse whom I had taken prisoner before Lutter and who had chanced to hear of my capture.

When he asked the Lieutenant-Colonel about me and told him he wanted to see me because of what I had done to him before Lutter, his fellow victim seized him by the hand and led him to the room where I was, saying: 'There she is, the baggage, I intend to hand her over to my stable lads as soon as may be,' for he never doubted but that the Captain would be as eager as he was to take a cruel revenge of me. But that honest cavalier was quite differently minded. No sooner had he seen me sitting there in my misery than he began to sigh and shake his head.

I quickly realized that he was of a gentle disposition, so I fell upon my knees before him and begged him, by all his noble virtues, to have mercy on the wretch that I was and to protect me from further shame. He took my hand and raised me to my feet, saying to the Lieutenant-Colonel and his henchmen: 'Gentlemen and fellow officers, I beg of you! What have you done with this lady?' Here the Lieutenant-Colonel, who was already deep in his cups, interrupted him and exclaimed: 'What! A lady? A witch, that's what she is!' Whereupon the Captain replied: 'Forgive me, sir, but to my certain knowledge she is the natural daughter of brave old Count T., a valiant and upright soldier who has risked life and limb and forfeited lands and titles for the common good, and my most gracious Sovereign will scarcely approve this man's child being so maltreated, however often she may have captured an officer from one side or the other. I have good reason to believe that at this very hour her father is pressing the Imperial forces in Hungary more closely than many a commander in charge of a foraging party hereabouts.'—'Ho!' replied the Lieutenant-Colonel churlishly, 'How should I know of this? Why did she not open her mouth and speak up?' The other officers, however, knew the Captain well as a person not only of noble blood but also high in the King's favour. They therefore begged him most humbly to overlook the matter, seeing that it could not now be undone, and to deal with it discreetly so that evil might not befall them because of it. In return, they pledged him their faithful service with life and property whenever the occasion might offer.

Then they besought me on their knees to forgive them, but I was unable to answer them except with tears, and so I escaped, though cruelly ravished, from the clutches of these brutes into the care of the Captain, who treated me far more civilly than I deserved, for he furnished me with a servant and escort from his Danish company and sent me straightway, without so much as laying hands on me, to a castle he had lately inherited from his mother's sister, where I was tended and cosseted like a princess. And this deliverance I owed both to my beauty and to my nurse, who, without my knowledge or consent, had secretly told the Captain of my origin.

Chapter Thirteen

AT the castle I took my ease, fluffing and preening myself like a sparrow plucked half dead from a frozen pond to nestle by a hot stove or before the kitchen fire. For I had no other business there of any kind but to indulge and groom myself as does a war horse in winter quarters to prepare for next summer's campaign and its hardships. In this way I was soon restored to health and sleekness, and even began to yearn for my cavalier. Nor did I have long to wait, for he called on me while the winter nights were still long, being no less eager than I for the fray and equally reluctant to wait for spring's awakening before performing its traditional rites.

When he visited me he came with four servants, though I was allowed to see but one of them, and that the one who had first brought me to the castle. It is impossible to describe the warmth and compassion of his condolences for my unhappy lot, the ringing vows with which he assured me of his steadfast devotion, or the courtly compliments with which he lamented his enslavement—body and soul—to so fair a conqueror before Lutter. 'Most noble and beautiful lady,' he said, 'though you did, indeed, set free my body promptly enough, yet in my spirit

I remain entirely your slave, coming to you now with no other desire than to receive sentence of life or death from your fair lips. Of life, that is, if you will deign to have mercy on your most wretched captive and release him from the dark dungeon of his unrequited love by your all-embracing compassion; or of death if you deny him mercy and relief, or think him unworthy of your affection. When, like unto the gallant Penthesilea, you dragged me captive from the battlefield, then indeed did I know true bliss, and only when this husk of my body was seemingly set free did my true sufferings begin. For by my very release was I banished from the sight of her who still held captive my heart—a banishment all the more cruel since our engagement on opposite sides left me no hope of ever setting eyes on you again. This my profound sorrow vented itself in the countless sighs with which I pined after my adorable conqueror and which, unheard and unheeded, were quite wasting away my bodily substance, etc., etc.'

Such and similar turns of phrase did my swain employ to persuade me to something for which I yearned as much as he did. But having been through this school before and knowing full well that what is most easily gained is least esteemed I feigned to be of a very different turn of mind, bewailing my sad fate as his prisoner and the fact that my body was so utterly at his mercy. I confessed that I was more deeply beholden to him than any other gentleman on earth, for he had rescued me from my ravishers, and that I was therefore in duty bound to show the deepest gratitude for his valiant services. But if this debt was to be repaid with my honour in the guise of love, and if he had brought me to this place for no other reason, then I was at a loss to see what glory he hoped to gain in the eyes of the world or what gratitude from me by his generous actions. I implored him not to blemish his fair name as a man of chivalry by a deed which he might soon come to regret, or by holding a poor, weak and defenceless creature captive in his castle against her will; and with that I began to weep so bitterly as if I had been in deadly earnest, again according to the verses noted in an earlier chapter.

Indeed, to raise myself even higher in his esteem I offered him 2,000 rixdollars as a ransom, if he would but let me return untouched to whence I came. But he replied that his love for me was such that he would not exchange me for the whole kingdom of Bohemia, nor was he so much my inferior in birth and breeding that a marriage between us need raise insurmountable difficulties. And so we behaved like two pigeons which a fancier locks up in a coop for mating, which cavort and caper until they are quite exhausted before they reach an understanding. So we, too, disported ourselves until I judged the time ripe and my resistance sufficient, whereupon I became so tame and showed myself so submissive towards this young gallant, who had barely completed his twenty-second year, that I readily succumbed to his golden promises and yielded to all his desires. And so much did I please him that he stayed with me the whole of that first month, though no one knew the nature of his business at the castle except the afore-mentioned servant and an old housekeeper who had orders to address me as 'your ladyship'. In this way I became the living proof of the old proverb which says that a whore in a palace is as diverting a sight as a tailor on a horse or a louse on a bald pate.

My lover visited me often during the winter, and had his pride not been too strong, I do believe he would have hung up his sword for good. As it was, he felt compelled to do his duty by his father and his King, who prosecuted the war with much diligence but little success. Yet he came so often and took so little care to disguise his visits that his old father and mother became aware of them and began to wonder what kind of magnet was hidden in this castle which so persistently drew his weapons away from the war. They therefore made close inquiries about me, concerned lest their son should waste his substance on someone of little worth and end by being chained to a person from whom their noble family would derive scant honour. What they discovered persuaded them to nip the impending betrothal in the bud, but so circumspectly as to avoid doing me any bodily harm or offending my kin, in case I was indeed, as the housekeeper had told them, a Count's daughter and had a promise of marriage from their son.

The first move in this affair was for the housekeeper to warn me discreetly that my lover's parents had learned that their son kept a secret mistress, whom he intended to marry against his parents' will. To this they would on no account consent, having already promised him in marriage to the daughter of a noble family. They therefore intended to have me seized, though what else they proposed to do with me the housekeeper professed not to know. The old woman's hints frightened me a good deal, but I took care to hide my fear from her and pretended, on the contrary, to be delighted, as if the Grand Mogul of India himself were about, if not to protect, then at least to avenge me. For the rest, I put my trust in my lover's deep devotion to me and his faithful promises, of which I had proof almost weekly— not only in loving letters but also, with each, some precious gift or token. In answer to his letters I informed him of what the housekeeper had told me, and begged him to deliver me from such perils and to ensure that neither I nor my family suffered any indignity at the hands of his. This correspondence ended with the arrival of two servants clad in my lover's livery, who brought me a letter instructing me to accompany them at once to Hamburg, where he would make me his lawfully wedded wife, whether his parents liked it or not. Once the deed was done both his father and mother would have no choice but to give their consent and put a brave face on what could no longer be mended. I fell into the trap like a bear in search of honey, and travelled with my escort post haste, first to Wismar and thence to Hamburg, where the two servants vanished, leaving me to search at my leisure for my Danish cavalier and would-be bridegroom. Only then did I perceive that I had been hoist with my own petard and that the cheat had been cheated in her turn. Indeed, I was given to understand that I had better suffer my humiliation silently and with a good grace, and to give thanks to God that the fine bride-to-be had not been drowned in the sea on the way. If I tried any tricks I might yet discover to my cost that my lover's family was powerful enough, even in a large city where I might think myself secure, to deal with me according to my true deserts.

What was I to do? My marriage, and with it all my high-flown hopes and fancies, were dashed and quite undone. The confiding and affectionate letters I had so regularly sent my lover had all fallen into his parents' hands, and they in turn had written those that I received, with no other aim than to lure me to the plight in which I now found myself. For I was soon reduced to short commons and compelled, not altogether unwillingly, once again to earn my daily bread by nightly exercise.

Chapter Fourteen

I DO not know how my lover took it when he found me no longer at his castle; whether he laughed or cried. For my part I was sorry that I could no longer enjoy him, and I think that he, too, would have been glad of my favours yet awhile, had his parents not dashed the cup so suddenly from his lips.

It was about this time that Wallenstein, Tilly and Count Schlick descended on all Holstein and the surrounding Danish lands with a locusts' swarm of Imperial troops, whom the citizens of Hamburg and other towns and villages were compelled to supply with forage and munitions. There was therefore much coming and going in the city and I had no lack of customers to keep me busy. By-and-by I discovered that my adopted mother, though still with the army, had lost all my baggage except for a few pack horses, which put paid to what plans I had for the future. I was well suited in Hamburg, it is true, and could scarcely have hoped for a better berth, but since this happy condition could last no longer than the military occupation I had need to consider what was to take its place.

One day a young trooper called on me, and I, finding him very much to my liking, resolute and not without private means, set all my traps for him and left no hunter's ruse untried until I had quite ensnared him and made him so much my loving slave that he would happily have eaten lettuce straight from my hand. He swore that the Devil should take him if he did not marry me, and would, indeed, have carried me off to church in Hamburg there and then had he not required his Captain's consent. Nor, indeed, when he had presented me to the regiment, did he have any difficulty in obtaining it, so that thereafter he was but waiting for a suitable time and occasion to make our union lawful.

His comrades, meanwhile, marvelled that Fortune should have bestowed on him so pretty a young mistress, and most of them would gladly have stepped into his shoes. The soldiers of this victorious army, long accustomed to good living and rich booty, were so sleek and well-nourished in their abundance that most of them were more intent on the pleasures of the flesh and the satisfaction of their wantonness than on capturing prizes and foraging for victuals. Chief among them was my bridegroom's Corporal, a coxcomb with thoughts for little else but venery who had wellnigh made a profession of endowing his comrades with horns, and would have thought himself quite disgraced had he failed to seize such an opportunity and bring it to a successful issue. We were stationed at that time at the village of Stormaren, which had never before known the meaning of war and so was overflowing with good and plentiful fare which the soldiers took as their due, regarding the peasantry on whom they battened as no better than menials, cooks and servants. There were revels day and night, and each trooper in turn invited his fellows to partake of his host's table and cellar. My bridegroom was no exception, and the aforementioned Corporal planned his campaign to get under my skirts accordingly. He waited until one day my bridegroom was making merry at his billet with two companions who happened to be in league with the Corporal. Then he came and ordered him out to

F   81

mount guard with the colours, so that he himself might make merry with me in his absence. But my bridegroom was not slow to see through this ruse, and since he would yield his place to no one or (to put it more bluntly) had no intention of being cuckolded by the Corporal, reminded him that there were several others whose turn of duty preceded his. The Corporal, however, cut him short and told him to obey his orders, or he would chase him to his post of duty quickly enough, for he was quite determined to have me there and then. My lover, on the other hand, had no intention of letting him, and persisted in his refusal until the Corporal drew his sword and swore that he would either see him go on guard or, by right of his authority, so mark him that all would henceforth know what obedience they owed him. But, alas, my lover took this in bad part, drew his own sword and dealt the Corporal such a clout on the head that all his lecherous and over-heated blood began to seep away and his lust was quite quenched, so that there was no need for me to fear him any longer. The two guests heard the Corporal's cries for help and fell upon my bridegroom with their weapons. He ran one of them through and drove the other out of the house, but this one returned presently, bringing with him not only a surgeon to tend the wounded, but also several other fellows who seized me and my lover and brought us before the Provost, where we were chained hand and foot. They gave my lover short shrift, hauling him before a court martial next day. And though the evidence left no shadow of a doubt that the Corporal had ordered him on guard for no other reason than to supplant him in my bed for the night, yet the sentence, for discipline's and order's sake, was that he should be hanged, and I whipped, for being the cause of the affray. In the end, however, they so far relented as to let him be shot and me escorted from the regiment's lines by the hangman, which made a sorry and degrading procession.

Yet sorrowful as this journey was for me, two troopers of the regiment decided to turn it to their profit—and mine, too, as they impertinently flattered themselves. I had been on my way scarcely more than an hour when I encountered them lurking in a thick wood through which I had to pass and where they hoped to give me a warm welcome.

Now though I must own that I have never in my life been so nice as to refuse a lusty lad his pleasure if the mood was upon him, yet these two knaves were out to take advantage of my sorrow and to have of me by force that for which I had just been banished and my lover shot. So I decided to resist them, and this the more so as I suspected that when they had had their will with me and done what they wanted they would go on to rob me—a design that I could almost read from their eyes and faces as they came fiercely at me with swords drawn, intending to frighten me into submission. But I, knowing that their keen blades could harm my skin no more than a pair of hazel switches, grasped a knife in each hand and set upon them so furiously that the first had a blade in his heart before he knew where he was. The other was stronger and more wary, and for a while neither of us could gain the upper hand. As we fought we flung insults at each other, he calling me a whore, a slut, a witch and even a devil, while I cursed him for a knave, cut-throat, robber and whatever other honourable names came to my mind. This uproar attracted a musketeer to us through the undergrowth, who stood for some time watching our strange combat, not knowing which of the two to succour and support. As soon as we became aware of his presence each of us appealed to him for help, and it needs no great wisdom to guess that Venus soon prevailed over Vulcan in this contest for the favours of Mars. I was quick to offer him pots of gold and dazzled him with my sweetest smiles.

He primed his musket, took aim at my assailant and threatened him until he turned his back on me and began to run so fast that he nearly lost his boots, leaving his dying companion to wallow in his blood at our feet. When the trooper had gone and we found ourselves alone together, the young musketeer seemed struck dumb by my beauty and hardly had the courage to ask me more than what fate had brought me all alone to this encounter with the troopers. So I told him everything that had happened to my late bridegroom, the Corporal and myself; about the two troopers, one dead and the other in flight, who had intended to ravish a poor deserted wretch by force, and how, as he had seen in part, I had given a good account of myself. I begged him, my rescuer and comforter, to continue to aid and protect me until such time as I might find shelter and asylum with honest folk, for which, as I did not fail to mention, he should receive a just and generous reward. Then he searched the dead man and took from him whatever he had of value, finding himself well rewarded for his pains, and the two of us made off in haste, walking as fast as our legs would carry us to put the wood behind us, and by nightfall reached the musketeer's regiment, which stood ready to move with Colalto, Altrinniger and Gallas to Italy.

Chapter Fifteen

HAD I but had a single honest vein in my body I might at that
time have arranged my affairs differently and set my life on an
honest course. For my mother by adoption, with the two of my
horses that were left and a small sum of ready money, found her
way to me and wisely counselled me to withdraw from the war
to my treasure in Prague or to the Captain's estates, and there
to live in peace and thrifty contentment. But young and reckless
as I was I would listen neither to wisdom nor reason and
continued on my giddy way, the madder the merrier. My
mother and I were staying with a pedlar attached to the very
same regiment in which my husband who had perished at
Hoya had been Captain. I was treated with some courtesy there
for his sake, and I do not doubt that I could have got myself
another stalwart officer for a husband if only we had been at
ease in some comfortable billet.

But as our host of 20,000 men, made up of three different
armies, was hurrying towards Italy and had to force its way
through Grisons in Switzerland (where we encountered many
obstacles) few men of sense gave any thought to courting, and

so I continued in my widowed state. I also discovered that some lacked the courage to ask for my hand in marriage while others had other reasons for holding back. But as for any suggestions of irregular or illicit favours, they believed me far too virtuous for it in view of my behaviour with my last husband, which had given me a better reputation than I deserved.

Yet if this prolonged fast was not much to my taste, the young musketeer who had come to my aid in the encounter with the troopers suffered far worse. He had conceived such a passion for me that it gave him no rest by day or night and he sought my company whenever time and his duties permitted. I knew full well what ailed him and where the shoe pinched, but as he lacked the courage to reveal his intentions to Courage, I despised him as much as I pitied him. Yet by-and-by I began to have doubts about my proud resolve to marry none but an officer. When I considered the pedlar's trade and had daily proof of what profit there was in it and how, contrariwise, many a gallant officer had to tighten his belt, I began to wonder how I might establish and manage such an enterprise myself. I made a tally of the money I had with me, which included a goodly number of gold coins sewn into my clothes, and found that it would be ample for the purpose. Only the thought of the shame of it still prevented me—of descending from the level of an officer's wife to that of a huckstress. But when I recalled that I was an officer's wife no longer, and very likely would never be one again, the die was cast, and in my imagination I was already drawing beer and wine from the barrel for sale at twice its cost and haggling and chaffering more fiercely than any old Jew.

Just at this time, as our treble army was crossing the passes through the Alps and descending into Italy, my gallant's passion reached its peak, without his ever having uttered so much as a word of it to me. One day he came to my pedlar's tent under the pretext of drinking a cup of wine, looking as wan and disconsolate as a woman just delivered of a child for which she can find neither a father nor milk and porridge. Yearning glances and heavy sighs were all he could muster in lieu of words, but when I asked him what ailed him he took his courage in both hands and exclaimed: 'Ah, my dearest lady (for he dared not address me by my nickname), if I told you what ails me it would so greatly affront you that you would either withdraw your gracious countenance from me for ever or wither me with the rebuke my audacity deserves. And the one would serve as well as the other to complete my unhappiness and drive me to my grave.' With that he fell obstinately silent once more. I answered: 'If either of these events can cause your death, then their opposites may serve to revive you. And since I am beholden to you for rescuing me from my assailants when we met outside Hamburg I would never willingly deprive you of the sight of my countenance for as long as you please; so be of good cheer.'—'Ah, my most gracious lady,' he began again, 'this is the very paradox of my present condition: for whereas this my sickness dates from the moment I first set eyes on you, yet now it would be death to me never to see you again. Truly a strange and unhappy predicament in which to find myself as a result of rescuing your ladyship from her peril!' I replied: 'Then I must be guilty of great perfidy, thus to have requited good with ill.'—'By no means,' said the musketeer, and I: 'What then is your complaint against me?'—'Not against you,' he said, 'but against my sorrow, my fate, perhaps my presumption, my reveries or I know not what! I cannot complain that your ladyship has been ungrateful, for the small trouble it cost me to drive off the remaining trooper who threatened your ladyship's honour was amply rewarded by what I found on the other, whom your gracious ladyship had already so valiantly slain in defence of her most precious virtue. My dearest lady,' he continued, 'the confused state I am in so confuses me that I can explain neither my confusion, nor what ails me, nor my or your accusations, or rather my innocence, or whatever might give me solace. Behold, my fairest mistress, I die because my lack of fortune and lowly estate prevent me from revealing to you how happy it would make me to be your most humble servant.' I was dumbfounded to hear such words from a simple musketeer, and one still so young. Disjointed though they were, and proceeding, as he said, from a confused mind, yet did they seem to augur a lively spirit and sensible understanding, not unworthy of love and apt enough to serve me honestly in the huckster's enterprise which so much preoccupied my thoughts. So I was brief with the ninny and said: 'My friend, in the first place you call me your mistress and in the second place yourself my servant if only I would permit it. And thirdly you complain that you will die if I avert my countenance from you. By all these tokens I perceive that you may be deeply in love with me. Tell me then, how I can requite this love? For I have no wish to be thought ungrateful towards the saviour of my honour.'— 'By loving me in return,' replied my gallant, 'and to be found worthy of this would make me the happiest creature on earth.' I said: 'It was you yourself who averred that you are of too humble a birth to aspire to the place by my side which you desire and your rambling speech seems to hint at. What then can be done to help you, to exonerate me from all charges of ingratitude and to cure you of your sickness?' He said that for his part he would gladly leave the decision to me, and this the more readily since he considered me a goddess rather than a human being, from whom he would unhesitatingly accept sentence of life or death, freedom or servitude, and, indeed, whatever I graciously deigned to decree. All this he affirmed with such manifest sincerity as to leave me in no doubt that here I had a fool at the end of a rope who in his self-abasement would rather strangle himself for my sake than live at liberty without me.

I decided to follow up my advantage and to strike while the iron was hot. And what else should I have done, seeing that the Devil himself does not scruple to ensnare those that find themselves as besotted as my would-be lover? Yet do I not say this in order to persuade honest Christians by my example to emulate the Evil One (as I did), but so that Simplicius (to whom I have dedicated these my memoirs) may understand what a fine lady it was he loved. And if you will but read on, my good Simplex, you shall discover that I repaid you for the tricks you played me in Griesbach a hundredfold, so that for every pound you gave you received a hundredweight in return. As for my gallant, I brought him to the point where he agreed to the following conditions, which he promised faithfully to obey.

First, he should buy himself out of his regiment, for in no other way could he become my servant, and I had no intention of becoming a musketeer's wife.

Secondly he was to live with me and show me all the love and duty which a husband shows his wife, the which I would requite.

Thirdly, however, such marriage was not to be consecrated in church unless and until I found myself with child by him.

Until then I would, fourthly, be and remain mistress not only of our joint wealth but also of my body and, indeed, of his, in all due form, as ordinarily a husband holds sway over his wife.

In view of this he should, fifthly, have no power to restrain or prevent me, or even give me sour looks, if I held converse with another man or engaged in any such traffic as commonly arouses a husband's jealousy.

And since, sixthly, I intended to establish a huckster's business, he should be its head, plying it with all due thrift and diligence at all times, but leaving to me the final decisions, in particular over the money and himself, and patiently suffer whatever blame I might see fit to attach to his conduct of the trade and to mend his ways accordingly. He was, in a word, to be the master to all outward appearances and to be treated as such by all the world, but in truth to owe me all the afore-mentioned duties and faithfully to observe them, and to this we plighted each other our troth.

Finally, in order to ensure that he would always remember his duty, he was, seventhly, to suffer me to call him by a special name which would consist of the first command I would give him.

When he had agreed to all these conditions and sworn to obey them, I sealed our contract with a kiss, but did not let him take any further liberties at that time. Soon afterwards he brought me his discharge from the regiment and I set about in earnest to establish myself as a well-found pedlar in another regiment, where I was soon driving bargains as if to the manner born.

Chapter Sixteen

MY young pedlar proved himself so amenable in all those tasks for which I had engaged and intended to use him, fulfilled the aforementioned conditions so punctiliously and showed himself so obedient that I had not the least cause for complaint. Indeed, if he could read a wish in my eyes it was as good as done, for so drunk was he with love for me that he seemed quite to have lost the use of his senses and altogether failed to comprehend, despite the evidence of his eyes and ears, what kind of a bargain he had of me and I of him. On the contrary, he firmly believed that he had won the most pious, faithful, sensible and chaste lover in all the world and this conviction my adopted mother (whom he held in great respect for my sake) did her best to foster—for my convenience as much as for his. She was more cunning than a vixen and greedier than a she-wolf, and I cannot make up my mind whether it was as a bawd or as a miser that she most excelled. If ever I felt a wanton desire but knew not how to indulge it (being much concerned for my reputation for piety and chastity) I had only to confide in her to have the matter arranged, for her conscience spread wider than the thighs of the Colossus of Rhodes, through which the largest ships could pass without striking their sails.

Once I conceived a burning desire for a young nobleman, who was then still an Ensign and who had been pursuing me with his attentions for some time. We had just set up camp outside a small town and my servants, together with most of the soldiers camping near us, had gone to fetch firewood and water. Some of the horses were tethered around our wagon, the rest grazing farther afield, and my young pedlar, who had just set up my tent, was busying himself about the wagon. It was at this untimely moment that my mother, whom I had but recently acquainted with my fancy, brought the Ensign to me. In the pedlar's hearing I asked him if he had the money with him and he, thinking I meant my whore's wages, said he had. Then I turned to the pedlar as if impatient at his slowness and said: 'Happy-go-Lucky that you are, away with you and fetch the piebald gelding from the meadow, for the Ensign has made a deal with me to pay for him on the spot and ride him away, and has no time to waste.' As my good lad set off obediently to carry out my first order, the old woman stood guard while the Ensign and I concluded our business to our great mutual satisfaction. The pedlar, as it turned out, found the horse far harder to catch than the Ensign the pedlar's wife, and when he returned to the tent quite worn out by the chase the Ensign made a great show of impatience because of the long delay. He later wrote a song about the affair called the Piebald Horse, which began: 'Ah, the ineffable pain' etc., and was sung for years all over Germany, although nobody knew its origin. As for my pedlar, he got the name of Happy-go-Lucky in accordance with our marriage contract, and this is the very same Happy-go-Lucky whom you, my good Simplicius, praise so highly and repeatedly in your memoirs as a splendid fellow. I would moreover have you know that all the tricks he helped you to play in Westphalia, at Philippsburg and elsewhere he learned from none other than me and my old mother, for when he first joined us he was as simple as any lamb, yet when we parted he was as crafty as a lynx and as sharp as vinegar.

Yet, truth to tell, he did not come by his cunning for nothing, but paid dearly for every lesson. Once, when he was still in his innocence, he, my mother and I were discussing the deceitfulness and wickedness of women, and he was so bold as to claim that no woman, however cunning, would ever get the better of him. Though this in itself was sufficient proof of his artlessness I felt that so reckless a claim touched my and all other sensible women's subtlety too closely to be dismissed in silence. I therefore told him plainly that if I had a mind to it I would undertake to deceive him no fewer than nine times before he had eaten his breakfast. He, for his part, averred that if I succeeded he would promise to be my slave and bondsman for the rest of his days. He was even so bold as to dare me to it, on the condition that if I failed to deceive him even once in that time I should let him take me to church for an honest wedding. When we had settled the wager on these terms I came to him next morning with a bowl of broth and a loaf of bread in one hand and a knife and a whetstone in the other, and asked him to sharpen the knife for me on the stone so that I might cut the bread into the broth. He took the knife and the stone from me and, having no water to hand, licked the stone with his tongue to moisten it. 'The Lord preserve us,' I exclaimed, 'that makes twice already!' He turned in surprise and asked me what I meant and I, in return, asked him whether he had already forgotten our wager of the previous night. He said he remembered it well, and asked in what way I thought I had deceived him. I answered: 'In the first place I blunted the knife on purpose so that you would have to sharpen it for me, and in the second I dragged the whetstone through a place you may readily guess and gave it to you to lick.'—'Enough, enough,' he cried, 'if that is the way of it you had better leave off and say no more, for I have no wish to know about the other seven times.'

So now I had my Happy-go-Lucky as a slave and bondsman;

93

my husband by night if nothing better offered, my servant by day, and at all times, in the eyes of the world, my lord and master. As for him, he knew so well how to play his part in the affair and to humour my every whim that I could have wished for no better husband as long as I lived. I would even have been glad to marry him had I not feared that he would thereafter shake off the yoke of obedience, claiming the sovereignty that would then be rightfully his and using it to pay me out a hundredfold for all the injuries I had done him in our un-wedded state and which must undoubtedly at times have made him grind his teeth. Meanwhile we continued to live together in the perfect harmony, if not the sanctity, of a pair of angels.

My mother minded the pedlar's store for me, I played the part of the pretty cook and serving wench whom a host keeps on his premises to attract clients, and my Happy-go-Lucky was master, servant, or whatever my whim demanded that he should be, obeying me in everything and heeding my mother's advice, but for the rest master over all my servants, of whom I had more than many a Captain. For the regiment's regular butchers were a careless and slovenly pack of ruffians who would rather spend their money on drink than earn more, which enabled me to bribe my way into their trade and keep two apprentice butchers, with whose help I gained the advantage over the regulars and finally drove them out of business. For I could always oblige any customer, wherever he came from, with every kind of meat, no matter whether he wanted it raw, boiled, roasted or on the hoof. As for stealing, looting and robbing (for which the fat, rich land of Italy was a veritable Paradise), Happy-go-Lucky and all my servants were required to risk their necks to do as much of it as was needful, and even Courage herself returned to her old trade and gave as good an account of herself as ever on the occasions when they encountered resistance. As a result, my purse grew so fat that I was able to send a bill of exchange for a thousand crowns to Prague wellnigh every month, though none of us ever went short of anything in camp. As far as that was concerned, I made it my business to see that my mother, my Happy-go-Lucky, my other servants and especially my horses never lacked food, drink, clothing or fodder, even if I myself had to suffer, go naked and make do without a roof over my head by day or night. But in return I required them, for their part, to labour diligently at all times to increase my fortune, even at the risk of their lives.

Chapter Seventeen

so there, my good Simplicius, you may mark and learn that I was already your good comrade Happy-go-Lucky's mistress and teacher when you, for aught I know, were still minding your Dad's swine, and long ere ever you had wit enough to be another man's fool. So much, then, for your boast that you made a fool of me at the waters of Griesbach.

After the first siege of Mantua we settled for the winter in a gay little town where I soon found ample scope for the practice of my former trade. No feast or banquet was complete without Courage's presence, and wherever she appeared the Italian strumpets found themselves out in the cold. For the truth of the matter was that the Italians thought me a rare and dainty dish while the Germans felt at home with me because I spoke their language. As for me, I was as fond of the one as of the other, and despite my renowned beauty neither excessively aloof nor overly expensive. Nor did any man ever have cause to fear trickery at my hands, as they often had from the Italians. And so it came about that I poached from the Southern whores many a fine fellow who forsook their company for mine, and made many enemies among them.

One day a gentleman of substance, who had hitherto been a faithful vassal of the most notable of the local ladies, whom he had abandoned for my sake, invited me to dine with him. This woman was determined to recover her prize and to this end persuaded a furrier's wife to slip me a potion at dinner which so distended my stomach that it threatened to burst. The winds in my belly built up such a furious pressure that in the end they vented themselves with a fanfare that rang so sonorously around the table that I was covered in confusion. And once having found an exit they passed through it so impetuously one after the other that the thunder was like the salvoes of several regiments. But when I rose from the table to leave the room my body's movement caused an even more violent eruption, so that at least one or two blasts escaped me at every step, though they followed one another so swiftly that nobody could have counted them, and I do believe their number, neatly and properly spaced, would have seen a diligent drummer through a two hours' march. Yet the whole business lasted no more than about half an hour, during which time both guests and servants suffered more pain from laughing than I from the incessant salvoes.

I regarded this trick as a deep disgrace and in my shame and anger would gladly have left the company had not my host, who had invited me for other purposes than the making of such sweet music, prevailed on me to stay. He appeared as indignant as I was, and swore by all that was holy that he would avenge this affront if only he could discover what brewer of pepper-corns and ants' eggs had caused so doleful a symphony. I was in some doubt whether to believe his protestations or to suspect him of having arranged the whole affair himself, but decided to brazen it out, looking around me with flashing eyes which, if looks could kill, would have left no one at the table alive to tell the tale. But in the end I learned from one of those present that the aforementioned furrier's wife was adept at concocting such potions and that, having seen her below stairs, he could not doubt but that she must have been persuaded to this trick by some jealous lady, with the aim of lowering me in the esteem of some cavalier. This seemed the more likely as she had already done a similar thing on a previous occasion to a rich merchant, who had lost (or, more aptly, blown away) his mistress' favours with the music which he had vented before a distinguished company. This explanation convinced me, and I bethought myself of some swift revenge, which must be both secret and unbloody, for we were under orders to be of good behaviour in our winter quarters, conquered though they were from the enemy.

When I had established that the business had indeed occurred in the manner my fellow guests had suspected, I closely studied the habits of the lady who had laid the trap for me, her comings and goings and all she did. When I was shown a window from which it was her custom to give audience at night to those who desired to visit her I acquainted two officers with the grudge I bore her and bade them carry out my revenge on pain of never enjoying my favours again. I insisted that they should carry out my instructions to the letter, for I thought it fitting that she, having vexed me with foul odours, should be rewarded with nothing less than the filth which was their origin. And this I arranged as follows: I had a cow's bladder filled with the most disgusting ordure to be found at the bottom of the privies and tied to a supple pole or rod of the kind used for beating walnut trees or sweeping chimneys. Armed with this weapon one of my two officers hid at night outside her house, and when the other began to spoon with the trollope as she leaned from her accustomed audience window, flung it at her face so violently that the bladder burst and the mess gushed all over her eyes, nose, mouth and bosom and dripped down on her finery and trinkets. Then the spooner and the executioner both took to their heels, leaving the whore to wail at the window as long as she pleased.

As for the furrier's wife, this is how I paid her out: her

husband was in the habit of collecting any hairs he found, even the cat's, as carefully as if they had been shorn from the Golden Fleece in Colchis. When he had gathered together a pound or two of this fluff he would take it to the hatter's who gave him a few pence for it, which helped to keep the fires burning and, though it was little enough, yet came conveniently on occasion. This I learned from an old furrier who had made a lining for my coat that winter. I therefore collected all the hairs and fluff I could find, shredded the stuff small, mixed it with tallow and got my lad to spread the mess around the furrier's privy. When the old skinflint saw the lumps of spoilt hair he took them for his own and had no other thought but that his wife had thus abused and ruined them. So he began to scold her as furiously as if she had undone and betrayed all Mantua and Casale, and as she denied her guilt as stubbornly as a witch under torture and even answered him tartly, he finally belaboured her hide as soundly as those of any of the wild and rare animals— not to mention household cats—which he was accustomed to tan. All of which pleased me so much that I would not have forgone the satisfaction of it for a dozen ducats.

There now only remained the apothecary who, as I suspected, had concocted the prescription which had caused me to make such base music, for he kept song-birds whose nourishment is reputed to cause the tumult to which I have referred. But he was well regarded by the officers, both high and low, for he ministered daily to our sick, and especially those with whom the Italian air disagreed. I, too, might have need of his services any day, and so I dared not provoke him too openly. Yet though my stomach had long since digested the potion, I still found it hard to digest the injury done me until I had avenged it in full. The apothecary had under his house a small, vaulted cellar in which he used to keep all manner of stores which needed a cool place for their preservation. Into this I directed the water from a nearby well through a long ox gut, one end of which I tied to the water spout, leaving the other to hang into the cellar through the window. Then I had the well water run into the cellar throughout the long winter night. Next morning the cellar was full to the brim with water, on which there floated a few small barrels of Malvasier and Spanish wine and other lighter objects. As for the rest, it lay spoilt six foot deep under water, and since I had made sure the ox gut was removed before daylight, it was commonly supposed that either the cellar had sprung a source overnight or that the apothecary had been tricked by witchcraft. But I knew the truth and gloated over my success when I saw the apothecary mourning over his spoilt wares. And in this affair, once again, the name of Courage stood me in good stead, for had it not been so well established some worthless rogue would doubtless have dubbed me Mistress Fart for the verve and spirit of my performance.

Chapter Eighteen

so greatly did I relish the profit which accrued to me from my manifold ventures that I grew more greedy for it day by day. Already it was all one to me whether I came by it honourably or shamefully; soon I began to care as little whether my business prospered better with God's help than with Mammon's, and in the end I threw conscience and decency to the winds in its pursuit by frauds, swindles and tricks so long as it increased my wealth. I turned my Happy-go-Lucky into a crooked horse dealer and taught him what wiles he did not already know, using every ruse, imposture and knavery ever practised in the trade. No merchandise, whether of gold, silver or jewels (not to mention pewter, copper, cloth, apparel or whatever else it might be), was too precious or too mean for my huckstering, and any who did not know where to turn their possessions, however acquired, into ready money were as sure of a welcome from me as thieves are from a Jew, who is concerned for their protection rather than their punishment. So it came about that my two carts resembled a rag-bag rather than a jewel casket, making it easy for me to relieve every soldier, high and low, of his money in exchange for anything that happened to take his fancy. But in return I had to spend a fair sum of money on gifts and bribes in order to protect myself and my dealings. The Provost was like a father to me, his old wife a mother, the Colonel's wife my kind patron and the Colonel himself my gracious lord, all of them serving me as a hedge against those who might wish to do me, my retinue or my business an ill turn.

One day an aged chicken thief (or rather, old soldier), who had plainly first shouldered his musket long before ever the troubles in Bohemia started, brought me an object in a sealed glass somewhat resembling a spider or a scorpion, but not exactly like either. I doubted whether it was an insect or indeed any other living creature, for there was no air in the glass which could have kept it alive, but took it rather for the invention of some subtle craftsman who had fashioned it as I know not what symbol of perpetual motion, for the thing was constantly moving and scrabbling around in its transparent prison. It pleased me greatly, and as the old man offered it me for sale I asked him how much? His price for the trifle was two farthings and I paid him on the spot, offering him a draught of wine into the bargain which he refused, saying that I had already paid what I owed him. This surprised me in so seasoned a toper, and I questioned him closely concerning his reasons for declining the drink with which it was my habit to seal even the meanest of bargains. 'Look you, Mistress Courage,' he replied, 'this glass is not like other merchandise. Its price, both for buying and selling, is fixed, and I advise you, when you decide to rid yourself of it, to sell it at less than the price you paid for it.'—'Then would I gain little from the bargain!' I exclaimed. 'As for that,' he said, 'it is your affair. For my part I have kept it by me for thirty years or more and never been the poorer for it, though I bought it for three farthings and sold it for two.' I could make nothing of this tale, or perhaps had no wish to probe it further, for I was just then preparing myself for some revels and the proper reception of several ambassadors of Venus, and the old droll's ramblings seemed to me of little account. I did not take him for the kind of man to get the better of Courage and so, secure in the knowledge that shrewder men than he had often sold me for a ducat what was worth a hundred, I pocketed my new treasure.

Next morning, when I awoke from my revels, I found it in my trouser pocket (for it was my habit always to wear trousers and jerkin), remembered how I had come by it and straightway put it with my other treasures, such as jewels and rings, to keep it safely until such time as I chanced upon some learned person who might instruct me as to its nature and purpose. But when, later in the day, I happened to put my hand into my pocket I found the glass there again, and no longer in the place where I had put it. More startled than frightened, I decided to find out more about it and hunted high and low until I found the old trooper again. I asked him what it was he had sold me, told him about its strange behaviour and pressed him to give me a full account of the trinket's character and powers. He replied: 'It is an obedient spirit, Mistress Courage, that brings much luck to whoever buys and keeps it. It reveals hidden objects, attracts clients for all manner of business and brings prosperity. It makes its owner beloved of his friends and feared by his foes, it renders him as impregnable as steel and preserves him from imprisonment. It grants good fortune and victory and ensures the goodwill of neighbours.' In fact, the old fox told me such a tale that had I believed him I might have thought myself more blessed than Fortunatus with his sack and his wishing cap. But I readily guessed that this so-called obedient spirit would not do me all these favours for nothing, and so I asked the old soldier what I, in return, would have to do for it, for I had heard that necromancers who use so-called mannikin-gallows to fleece their victims are obliged to pay the mannikin homage with weekly ablutions and other rituals. The old soldier replied that nothing of the kind was needed in this case. Such a mannikin was something quite different from the object I had bought from him. I retorted that nevertheless it would doubtless not be my servant and fool

103

for nothing, and that he should tell me plainly and honestly whether I could have it without risk or payment of reward, and enjoy such splendid services without any return or obligation on my part. 'Mistress Courage,' he replied, 'this is all you need to know: that when you would be rid of it you must sell it for less than you paid for it. I told you this plainly when you struck your bargain with me. Let others answer the question "why?",' and with that he went his way.

In those days my Bohemian mother was my closest confidant, my father confessor, my favourite, my friend and faithful counsellor. There was nothing that I concealed from her, and so I also consulted her about the treasure I had purchased. 'Indeed,' she said, 'it is a spiritus flammarum ['familiaris' was no doubt the word she meant and intended to use] which will perform all that the old soldier promised. But whoever keeps it until his death must take it with him over to the other side, which, as its name implies, will doubtless be to Hell, which reportedly is full of fire and flames. And this is why it can only be sold more cheaply than it is bought, so that at last no more buyers can be found for lack of a coin small enough for the purchase. As for you, my daughter, you stand in the direst peril, for you will be the last who can sell it. Yet what fool will buy it from you, knowing that he cannot sell it in his turn and is therefore buying his very soul's damnation from you?' It was clear enough to me what a bad bargain I had struck, but I was in the flower of my youth and my reckless spirits consoled me with the expectation of a long life and made me trust in the world's wickedness, so that I took it lightly enough, saying to myself: 'Enjoy this aid, this prop, this auspicious fortune as long as you can, and no doubt one day you will find some careless fellow somewhere who in his cups, or from poverty, despair, blind hope of fortune, or for greed, lechery, anger, envy, revenge or whatever will rid you of this visitor at the appointed price.'

So I availed myself of the spirit's help in every way and by every means, as I had been instructed by the old soldier and by my former nurse and adopted mother, and had every opportunity of observing its daily blessings. Where another sutler tapped a single cask of wine I sold three or four, guests who had eaten or drunk at my table never failed to return. Any man I set eyes upon and desired I found instantly ready to serve me with the utmost vigour and to worship me almost as if I were a goddess. Whenever I entered a billet whose owner had fled, or some other shelter or abandoned dwelling which none would live in (regimental butchers and pedlars rarely being quartered in palaces) I would instantly discover whatever it contained of value and find, by I know not what inner flair, treasures on which the sun had not shone for a hundred years or more. Yet I cannot deny that there were those who would have nothing to do with me, but despised and even persecuted rather than honoured me. And I have no doubt that these were the people who were guided by a more powerful spirit than that which protected me. Though it gave me much food for thought and prompted me to some contemplation and revery upon the why's, how's and wherefore's, yet was I already so steeped in greed and its attendant vices that I was content to leave matters as they were and made no effort to alter the shaky foundations on which my salvation rested. And so my fortune continued to grow until it almost made me afraid.

All this, my good Simplici, I relate for your edification, since in your memoirs you boasted of having enjoyed the favours of a lady at Griesbach, yet knew so little of her. I would also have you note that if you had been a man of sound sense at the time of our amorous encounter there, you would have avoided my snares as surely as those who enjoyed the good Lord's protection when I was in possession of my familiar spirit.

Chapter Nineteen

THERE is another thing you should also know, Simplicius: it was not only I who pursued these evil ways, but I dragged my Happy-go-Lucky, whom you, in your memoirs, describe so fondly as your best companion and an honest fellow, in my wake. Nor was there anyone to prevent it or, indeed, to give it a second thought. For is it not common for wives to make their husbands accomplices in crime, whether by threats or by blandishments, even though their marriage vows contained no such solemn undertakings as Happy-go-Lucky had entered into in our covenant? Therefore mark and learn.

While we were investing the famous city of Casale, Happy-go-Lucky and I drove to a neutral frontier town near by to buy victuals for our camp. It was my habit, on these forays, not only to huckster like a shrewd descendant of the Tribes of Israel, but also to seek profit from the trade of the Cytherean virgins. I was accordingly bedizened like Jezebel, not caring whether it should fall to Ahab's or Jehu's lot to seduce me. To promote a speedy consummation I entered a church, for I had been told that in Italy amorous intrigues were hatched and pursued in these sacred precincts, they being the only places where beautiful and charming women were allowed to appear in public. I found myself standing beside a young lady and at once became involved with her in a contest of looks and apparel, for I noticed that a man who gave her many a fair smile never so much as glanced in my direction. I confess that it vexed me much to see her so greatly preferred, and myself neglected for such a bean-stalk of a woman. This annoyance and the thoughts of revenge it provoked were my chief devotions during this divine service. While it was still in progress, my Happy-go-Lucky appeared at my side, though why I cannot imagine. It could scarcely have been love of God that had drawn him there, for this was not one of the lessons I had taught him, nor was he born or brought up to it by the study of holy writ or attendance at pious sermons. Nevertheless, there he was at my elbow, very handy to listen to the whispered instructions I gave him to follow my rival and find out where she lived, so that I might obtain possession of an emerald of surpassing beauty which she wore at her throat.

He did his duty like the faithful servant he was and returned with the intelligence that she was the well-born wife of a rich merchant who had his palace near the market square. I thereupon informed him that he need expect no further favours from me nor, indeed, would I permit him so much as to touch me, until he had deposited the emerald in my hands, for which purpose I would put at his disposal all necessary means, devices and stratagems. Though he began by scratching his head and vowing that my demands were beyond all reason and impossible to meet, yet when he saw me adamant he declared that he would obey me even unto death.

That, my good Simplicius, is how I trained your Happy-go-Lucky, almost like a young setter, and though, to tell the truth, he possessed a natural bent for knavery, possibly even exceeding your own, yet would he never have become so accomplished a knave but for my schooling.

It so happened that my hammer, which I used both as a

weapon and as a key to open any peasants' chests and cabinets that resisted gentler persuasion, had recently been fitted with a new shaft. It was my practice to have these shafts hollowed out to a width which would accommodate either ducats or lesser coins of the same size. For since I was no longer permitted to bear a sword and had given up carrying a pair of pistols, I always kept this hammer by me, and my aim was to have it stocked inwardly with ducats that might stand me in good stead during the hazards of war. When this new shaft was finished I tested the width of its bore with some Swiss coins I had brought with me to exchange into other currency. The hollow was just wide enough to take them, though it required some slight pressure—somewhat less than for packing the charge of a musket. I did not have enough of these coins to fill the shaft and was diverted, when holding the hammer by the head and using it as a stick, to hear a muffled click as now one and then another fell to the bottom, much to the astonishment of anyone within earshot, who had no notion whence it came. But enough of lengthy descriptions: I gave Happy-go-Lucky my hammer, and with it exact instructions how to use it in order to get me my emerald.

Happy-go-Lucky now disguised himself, donned a periwig, wrapped a borrowed cloak about his person and did nothing all day but stand opposite the lady's palace, studying the edifice from top to bottom as if he intended purchasing it. I had also hired by the day a drummer boy who was so sharp that you could have used him to season vinegar. He had no other duty but to roam around the square and wait until such time as Happy-go-Lucky might have need of him, for this downy bird spoke Italian as well as he did German, which Happy-go-Lucky did not. I for my part had a liquid solvent prepared by an alchemist (its name is nothing to the purpose) which ate through any metal in a matter of hours, softening it to a paste or even dissolving it altogether. This I applied to some stout bars outside a cellar window belonging to the palace. When three days had passed and Happy-go-Lucky still stood gazing at the house like a cat at a new barn door, the lady at last sent a servant out to him to inquire what he meant by his vigil and hoped to gain from the contemplation of her house. Happy-go-Lucky summoned the drummer and made him explain in Italian that so vast a treasure lay buried there, which he alone could raise, that he undertook to make the whole town rich with it. The lady, on hearing this, invited both Happy-go-Lucky and the drummer into the house and, when she had heard his lies about the treasure from his own lips, was consumed with desire to possess it and asked the drummer what manner of man Happy-go-Lucky was, whether a soldier, whence he came, etcetera. 'No,' replied the double-dyed rogue, 'he is something of a necromancer as you might say, who follows the troops only in order to discover hidden treasure. He has found, so I've been told, whole barrels and chests full of money in old castles in Germany.'

To cut a long story short, after much talk the fruit was ripe for plucking and it was decided that Happy-go-Lucky should search for the treasure. He asked for two consecrated candles and himself produced a third which he had on him and which could be extinguished at will by means of a brass wire that ran through it. With these three candles the lady, two of her servants, Happy-go-Lucky and the drummer wandered through the house, the master being absent. Happy-go-Lucky had told them that his candle would go out of its own accord wherever the treasure was hidden. When the strange procession had ranged high and low, Happy-go-Lucky muttering incomprehensible words as he shone his candle into every nook and cranny, they came at last to the cellar where I had treated the iron window bars with my lotion. Here Happy-go-Lucky stood facing a wall and, after going through his accustomed ritual, pulled the brass wire to extinguish the candle. 'There, there,' he said through his drummer-interpreter, 'the treasure lies behind yonder wall.' Then he muttered some more mysterious gibberish and struck the wall several times with the hammer, making the coins in the handle rattle at each blow. 'Did you hear that?' he said. 'The treasure is in full bloom, which happens but once every seven years, and now is the time to raise it while the sun still stands in the sign of the hedgehog. If we tarry, another seven years must elapse before it can again be attempted.'

Now the lady and her servants would have sworn a thousand oaths that the tinkling noise had issued from the wall, and therefore never questioned Happy-go-Lucky's tale. The lady urged him to raise the treasure there and then, in return for an appropriate fee which she asked him to name. He, however, gave her to understand that in cases of this kind it was his custom neither to ask for nor to accept any fee other than what it might please the beneficiary to give him. The lady did not insist but assured him that she would so reward him as to give him no cause for complaint.

He then asked for seventeen selected grains of incense, four wax candles sprayed with holy water, eight ells of scarlet cloth, a diamond, an emerald, a ruby and a sapphire, all of which must have adorned a lady's neck both as virgin and wife. He also made it a condition that he should be locked up in the cellar by himself, the key to remain in the lady's own hands, to assure both her of the safety of her cloth and jewels, and him of freedom from interruption and noise. Then he and the drummer were served a sumptuous meal and the drummer given a reward for his services as interpreter, while the objects asked for were assembled. At last Happy-go-Lucky and all his tackle were locked in the cellar from which it seemed impossible for a man to escape, for the window or skylight that gave on to the square was not only high up in the wall, but also well secured by the aforementioned stout bars. As for the interpreter, he was dismissed and came straight to me and told me all that had happened.

At the time of night when most people are in their deepest sleep Happy-go-Lucky and I set to work. I broke away the iron bars as easily as if they had been turnip chips, lowered a rope to Happy-go-Lucky in his cellar and pulled him up with all his loot, among which, sure enough, I found my splendid emerald.

I was glad of the prize, but not so glad by far as of the successful outcome of my stratagem. The drummer had made haste to leave the town the previous night, but Happy-go-Lucky next day disported himself calmly among a throng of citizens all abuzz with the exploit of the cunning thief, while at the gates the guards searched every stranger in the hope of finding the culprit. That, my good Simplicius, was how your Happy-go-Lucky's skill was sharpened by me and exerted at my behest. Nor do I tell you this otherwise than as a single example out of many. For if I were to recount all the tricks and knaveries which I compelled him to carry out for my sake, droll though many of them were, I'll wager that both you and I would soon tire of the tale. Indeed, were I to treat of all these things as broadly as you described your fool's errands in your memoirs, this would become a thicker tome even than yours, though no doubt a more diverting one. However, I will give you a few more instances.

Chapter Twenty

WHEN it became clear that our siege of Casale would be prolonged many of the camp followers began to build themselves
huts, in order to live in greater comfort than in tents while it
lasted. Among the sutlers in the army's train there were two
Milanese who had made themselves a cabin out of wooden
planks for the safer storage of their merchandise, which consisted of shoes, boots, ruffs, shirts and other clothing for
officers and common soldiers, both mounted and on foot. Their
trade, as I saw it, was doing mine much damage and injury,
for they were fleecing the soldiers, at half or a quarter of its
true value, of much loot, silverware and jewellery which in
their absence would have accrued to my profit. Lacking the
power to put a stop to their business altogether, I decided at
least to take a usurer's toll of it.

The lower part of the cabin contained their merchandise
and also served as a shop. In the loft under the roof they had
their sleeping quarters, which they reached by means of a
ladder of some seven or eight rungs. In the floor of the loft
they had left a large hole, for the easier discovery of any night-
time intruder, and to allow them to give him a warm welcome

with their pistols, of which they had many. When I had assured myself that the door of the shed would open without much noise I laid my plans very simply. I made my Happy-go-Lucky gather me a bundle of sharp thorns, some six feet long and as many as a man could carry in his arms. I myself filled a large brass clyster with sharp vinegar, and thus equipped we made our way to the cabin at dead of night. I had no trouble in opening the door noiselessly, having previously made a thorough inspection of it, and when this had been accomplished Happy-go-Lucky leant the bundle of thorns against the ladder, which led straight up to the loft without any kind of trap door at the top. The noise of this operation awakened the Italians and we could hear them stirring above us. Not doubting that their first move would be straight for the hole to see what was happening beneath, I placed myself accordingly and squirted the eyes of the first who appeared at the opening so full of vinegar that he was quickly cured of his curiosity. The other clambered down the ladder in his night shift and drawers and was at once so rudely welcomed by the thorns that, like his companion, he must have thought the Devil himself had entered the cabin and bewitched it with his baleful magic. In the meantime Happy-go-Lucky had seized a bundle of cavaliers' ruffs and made off with them. I contented myself with a bolt of linen, turned on my heels and slammed the door shut after me, leaving the two Italians to their distress, the one, no doubt, wiping his eyes yet awhile and the other disentangling himself from his thicket of thorns.

That, my good Simplicius, is how skilful I was and how, little by little, I trained Happy-go-Lucky. I stole, as you will have perceived, not for need or want, but mostly to avenge some slight, or to vex those who displeased me. Happy-go-Lucky, for his part, persevered as my pupil and became such a dab hand at the business that in the end he would have undertaken to steal anything you might like to name, even though it were chained and bolted to the firmament. Nor did I in the least grudge him his profit, but gladly let him keep his own hoard (for we used to share our loot equally), with which to do as he pleased. But being an incorrigible gambler he rarely amassed any great treasure. Though at times he had the makings of a fair fortune, his ill luck with the dice always parted him from it before long. But to me he remained ever faithful and obedient, and I could not have hoped to find a better slave anywhere on earth. Yet now you shall hear what it profited him, how I rewarded his services and how, in the end, I parted company with him.

Chapter Twenty-One

OUR regiment was moved from its billets in Casale to the siege of Mantua shortly before the fall of that city, and the move brought more grist to my mill than ever. There were more troops here than in our former camp, in particular more Germans who soon became my customers and gave me so much work that my wealth increased by leaps and bounds and I was able to send some sizeable bills of exchange to Prague and other German cities to swell my fortune. This prosperity and the lush daily pickings that I shared with my retainers, at a time when many went hungry and in want, gradually corrupted my Happy-go-Lucky, until he began to live the life of a squire. He spent his days eating, drinking, gambling and taking his ease, leaving the pedlar's store and whatever other opportunities there might be for turning a quick penny to look after themselves. He had, moreover, gathered a pack of worthless and spendthrift cronies about him who led him astray and spoilt him for all those enterprises in which I had trained and used him. 'Ho,' they said, 'do you call yourself a man and let that whore lord it over you and yours? It is not as if the shrew were even your wife, so that you had no choice but to suffer her. If I were in your shoes I would beat her until she came to heel, or send her to the Devil.' All this I heard betimes, much to my vexation and sorrow, and began to think of ways and means to send my Happy-go-Lucky packing, yet without giving him or his retinue the least inkling of my intentions. My servants (among them four strong lads employed as porters) were all loyal and true to me, the officers had their own reasons for protecting me, the Colonel himself was disposed in my favour and his wife even more so. Elsewhere I greased whatever palms I thought might help me in the domestic war which I expected Happy-go-Lucky to declare on me at any moment.

I knew full well that I needed him as a figure-head for my business, that as a man he provided the shield behind which I carried it on, and that without him I would very soon have traded my last. I therefore acted with great caution and gave him money every day—both for gambling and carousing—not in order to buy back his former loyalty but rather to render him careless, reckless and insolent towards me and to tempt him into some gross outrage which would manifestly make him unworthy of dominion over me and mine. In short, I wanted him to give me cause to part with him, for by this time I had grubbed and scraped so much money together, and had it so well secured, that I cared little for the pedlar's store or, indeed, for the whole war itself and whatever I might still gain from it.

But whether Happy-go-Lucky lacked the spirit to follow his cronies' advice and publicly demand his rights of me, or whether he was merely content to live in heedless and dissolute abandon I know not. At any rate he continued to show himself obliging and humble towards me and never gave me so much as an angry look, much less a hard word. Though I well knew the path along which his companions were urging him I could detect no hint in his actions of any desire to challenge my rule. Yet in the event it came about most curiously that he did offend me after

116

all and that, whether he liked it or not, we came to a parting of the ways.

One night as I lay safely asleep beside him, he, having just come home the worse for drink, suddenly struck me in the face with his fist as hard as he could, so that I awoke with the blood pouring from my nose and mouth, and so dizzy in my head that I marvelled that he had not knocked all my teeth down my throat. You may imagine the sermon I preached, calling him a murderer and whatever other honourable names came to my mind. But he replied: 'You bitch, why don't you give me my money which I have earned in the sweat of my brow?' and continued to thump me so that it was all I could do to ward off his blows. By now we were both sitting up in bed and wrestling with each other, and as he kept on demanding money from me I finally gave him a sound clip over the ear which stretched him out on his back again. Then I slipped out of the tent and set up such an outcry that not only my mother and servants, but also our neighbours awoke and came out of their huts and tents to see what was afoot. It so happened that most of them were on the staff, commonly lodged with the train behind the fighting soldiers, such as the Adjutant, Quartermaster, Provost, Sergeant-Major, Hangman, Whore-master and such like. At great length I told them my tale of woe, borne out as it was by my appearance, of how my fine husband had treated me thus without rhyme or reason. My fair bosom was spattered all over with blood, and Happy-go-Lucky's merciless fist had so dis-figured my comely features at a single blow that Courage was recognizable only by her plaintive and tearful voice, though none of those there assembled had ever before heard me weep or complain. They asked me for the cause of our quarrel and the encounter to which it gave rise, and when I told them exactly what had happened, all who heard it swore that Happy-go-Lucky must have gone out of his mind. But I for my part suspected that he had been put up to it by his cronies and boon companions, so as to filch from me, first my breeches, then my authority and in the end my hoard of money.

117

As we were standing there gossiping, and some of the women busying themselves to staunch the flow of blood from my face, Happy-go-Lucky came crawling out of our tent, joined us at the watch fire by the Colonel's baggage and could scarcely find words to express his remorse and to beg my and everyone else's pardon for his misdeed. He all but fell on his knees at my feet to obtain forgiveness and a renewal of my former grace and favour. But I stopped up my ears and would not hear or take note of anything he said, until our Lieutenant-Colonel returned from his rounds. To him he swore a great oath that he had dreamed he was sitting at the gambling tables where someone tried to cheat him of a sizeable stake. He had come to blows with him in his dream and so, entirely against his will and conscious intention, struck his dear, innocent wife in his sleep. The Lieutenant-Colonel was a cavalier who hated me and all other whores like the plague, but was well enough disposed towards my Happy-go-Lucky. So he sent me packing back to my tent with him, warning me to shut my gob or he would hand me over to the Provost or even have me whipped, as I had so long and amply deserved.

'A pox on you,' I thought to myself, 'for a lousy judge and a knavish sentence. But never fear, though you be the Lieutenant-Colonel and impervious alike to my beauty and my flattery, yet there are others, and more of them to boot, who will readily yield to both and do me justice.' So I kept as quiet as a mouse, but so did my Happy-go-Lucky, whom the Lieutenant-Colonel warned that if it happened again he would have him punished so unmercifully as to make him wish he had never started his nocturnal quarrels. To both of us he said that we had better make it up before morning, or he would have us before the Judge Advocate who would give us something graver to think about. So we went back to bed together, each with his bruises, for I had given Happy-go-Lucky as good as I got. Again he swore by all the saints that the story of his dream was true, but I told him that all dreams were without substance, though there had been nothing insubstantial about the blow I had received.

Then he tried to prove his love for me by deeds, but partly because of the blow and even more because of my desire to be rid of him I coldly rejected all his advances. Next day I gave him all the money he wanted for gambling and drinking, but few kind words, and to make sure he did not rob me of the small sum I kept by me to carry on our trade, I hid it with my mother and made her sew it safely into the clothes she wore next her skin, so that she was never parted from it, day or night.

Chapter Twenty-Two

IT was not long after this our midnight battle that the city of Mantua fell to a ruse of war, followed very soon by the signing of a peace treaty between the Imperial army of the Duke of Savoy and the French one under the Duke of Nevers. Indeed, it appeared as if our engagement had signalled the end of the Italian campaign, the French withdrawing from Savoy back to France, and the Imperial forces hurrying to Germany to see what the Swedes were up to. Willy-nilly I followed in their train, as if soldiering had indeed been my profession. For some weeks our regiment was stationed, either to recuperate or because the flux and even the plague were rife among us, in open country on crown lands near the river Thonau, where our comfort left much to be desired compared with the lush life of Italy. But I managed not too badly, with Happy-go-Lucky showing me a more than dog-like devotion so that, to outward appearances at least, I made my peace with him, though

120

secretly I was constantly on the watch for an opportunity to cast him off.

This my steadfast desire was fulfilled at last in the following manner, which shows how a careful, sensible and indeed innocent man, who awake and sober can hold his own against women, the world and the very Devil himself, may be undone by his own foolish frailty and plunged, by the stupor of drink or sleep, into irretrievable calamity and disaster.

Just as in my soul I now bore him a deep, abiding and relentless grudge for every smallest slight and fancied insult he inflicted on me, so my body, too, seemed incapable of mending and recovering from even the most paltry injury; but whether this was in sympathy with my mood or because my tender skin and delicate complexion could not withstand a severe drubbing as easily as an Austrian clod-hopper's I know not. Be that as it may, my usually comely face still bore the blue marks of Happy-go-Lucky's assault before Mantua, when he forgot himself once more in the aforementioned camp on the Thonau. As before, I was fast asleep when he seized me round the waist, threw me over his shoulder and carried me, clad only in my shift as he had found me, towards the Colonel's watch fire, with the evident intention of throwing me on to it. Befuddled with sleep as I was, I scarcely knew what was happening but sensed my peril, all naked and being borne swiftly by Happy-go-Lucky towards the fire. So I began to scream as if I had fallen into the hands of murderers, which roused the whole camp, the Colonel himself leaping from his tent sword in hand and other officers likewise, prepared to quell some violent riot (there being no present danger from the enemy) but finding only a ridiculous and foolish spectacle— for I should imagine we were a strange and diverting sight to behold. The guard closed in on Happy-go-Lucky before he could cast his reluctant burden into the flames, and when they perceived her to be naked and recognized her as his Courage to boot, the Corporal had the courtesy to throw a coat over my shoulders. Meanwhile a bevy of officers crowded around us, of

121

every rank and degree, holding their sides with laughter, the Colonel among them as well as the Lieutenant-Colonel who had but lately made peace between Happy-go-Lucky and me with his threats.

When Happy-go-Lucky at last feigned recognition of those around him, or else returned to his senses (for in truth I know not what went on in his mind), the Colonel asked him what he meant by his prank. He replied that he had had a dream in which his Courage appeared covered all over with venomous snakes and had intended to rescue and deliver her from them by dunking her in fire or water. With this in mind he had seized her and carried her off as they had all witnessed, for which he was most deeply and heartily sorry. But both the Colonel and the Lieutenant-Colonel who had taken his part before Mantua shook their heads, and as the joke was beginning to pall handed him over to the Provost for the night; and me they sent back to my tent to return to my rest.

Next morning our case came before the Judge Advocate and was soon settled, for pleas in wartime are wont to be shorter than in peace. Though all those present already knew that I was not lawfully wedded to Happy-go-Lucky, but only his mistress, I insisted on a proper and legal separation, saying that my life was no longer safe in bed beside him, with which all the assessors agreed, averring that it was sufficient reason to end even a lawful marriage. The Lieutenant-Colonel who had so firmly taken Happy-go-Lucky's part before Mantua now condemned him with equal severity, and all the other officers of the regiment were likewise on my side. When, in addition, I produced my written contract setting forth the terms of our association until marriage, and stressed the danger to life and limb which I would run by sharing bed and board with such a marriage partner, the Court pronounced that we be separated forthwith, on pain of certain forfeits, though it decreed that we were still committed to share between us whatever we had jointly earned. Against this I argued that it was contrary to our initial agreement, and that Happy-go-Lucky, since first he took up with me, or rather—to call the thing by its proper name—since first I befriended him and set him up to manage my store, had wasted far more than ever he had won, to which the whole regiment could bear witness. In the end the Court decided that in these circumstances, and with the two of us unable to come to an amicable agreement, the regiment would apportion our goods as it saw fit.

To this I readily gave my consent, and Happy-go-Lucky, too, was content to take what little the regiment was likely to award him, for since I was now paying him and the rest of my servants out of current profits and no longer so liberally as in Italy, putting them at times in imminent danger of having to tighten their belts, the poor ninny presumed that my money must be running out and that I had far less than in truth I had. Nor need this surprise anyone, for he never suspected how carefully and tenaciously I had been hoarding it.

It was at this very time, Simplicius, that the regiment of Dragoons to which you were apprenticed at Soest was being reinforced by numbers of young lads who had grown up in the service of officers of foot regiments and who, having reached man's estate, had no wish to become musketeers. This was Happy-go-Lucky's chance, and made him the readier to come to an agreement with me on the following terms: I gave him the best horse I had, with saddle and bridle, a hundred ducats in cash and the dozen cavaliers' ruffs he had stolen under my guidance in Italy and which we had not yet dared to display among our wares. It was also agreed that he would buy my familiar spirit from me for one farthing, and in this manner I fitted him out and cast him adrift. Soon now you shall also hear with what a fine present I endowed you. Have but a little more patience and listen first how Happy-go-Lucky rid himself of the object in the glass.

As soon as he had it he became arrogant beyond all measure and had but to look at a fellow, who had never in his life done him any harm, to want to be at his throat. He also gave himself out to be a duelling-master and knew how to find any kind of hidden treasure and all kinds of other secrets too numerous to relate. But when he discovered how dangerous a guest he was harbouring he cast about for ways of discarding it. However, since there was no smaller coin than that for which he had bought it, he could not sell it in his turn, so he tried to give it back to me. Once, when we met in the concourse of armies besieging Ratisbon, he even threw it at my feet, but I merely laughed, and with good cause, for far from wishing it success-fully back on me Happy-go-Lucky found it still in his knapsack when he returned to his quarters. I have been told that he threw the glass several times into the Thonau, but always found it again among his belongings. In the end he put it in a baker's oven and so rid himself of it. But as he carried the spirit around with him I began to feel uneasy about the whole business and turned all my belongings into ready money, dismissed my servants and retired with my Bohemian mother to Passau, to live in comfort on the proceeds of my hoard and to await the war's end, for I feared Happy-go-Lucky might go to law against me over the sale of the familiar spirit and have me sentenced as a witch.

Chapter Twenty-Three

PASSAU proved to be far less to my taste than I had expected. I found it much too pious for my liking and would have preferred to see more soldiers than nuns, and lusty young squires than monks. Nevertheless I remained there, for it was a time when not only Bohemia but well nigh all Germany sighed under the scourge of war. Seeing myself so constantly surrounded by the fear and love of God I even made an outward show of piety myself, and my Bohemian mother and one-time nurse had the good fortune of going the way of all flesh in this devout place and the lustre of her new-found godliness. I had her buried with as much pomp as if she had already been beatified, but took her death as an omen of future sorrow, for now I had no one left in the world to whom I could entrust my affairs with safety and honour. It was for this reason as well that I began to conceive a veritable hatred for the place which in all innocence had robbed me of my best friend, nurse and counsellor. Yet I curbed my impatience and stayed there until news came that Wallenstein had conquered Prague, the capital of my homeland, and restored it to the Imperial fold. This news, together with the threat of the Swedes, who had occupied Munich and all Bavaria, with Passau in daily dread of their approach, prompted me to return to Prague, where most of my treasure was also.

But scarcely had I installed myself comfortably and begun planning how to enjoy my ill-gotten gains in peace and contentment in this large and therefore, as it seemed to me, safe city when behold, Arnheim defeated the Imperial forces at Lignitz, with the capture of fifty-three standards, and straightway closely invested Prague. The most illustrious Ferdinand II, however, sent Gallas to the rescue (he himself being engaged in attacking Ratisbon), and by this succour not only was Prague relieved but the enemy driven out of Bohemia altogether.

It was then that I understood that neither great and mighty cities nor their walls, battlements and moats could protect me and my treasure from the warlike skill of those who lodged in the open, in huts and tents, and were free to roam and forage where they pleased. I therefore abandoned my plans for a settled life and considered how I might once again join a field army.

Though I had lost much of my former beauty, I was at that time still comely enough and smooth of face and body, and so, by diligence and long-practised wiles, I succeeded in discovering yet another Captain of foot among Gallas' troops who would marry me. It was almost as if the city of Prague owed it to me or in some other way felt obliged to provide me with husbands, and every one of them a Captain. Our wedding was celebrated in princely fashion, but the festivities had scarcely ended before we received orders to join the Imperial armies at Noerdlingen, with the Duke of Weimar and Gustavus Horn hastening to its relief. A bloody battle followed whose issue and consequences will not be forgotten as long as there are men alive to read history books. Though the battle's outcome was most auspicious in every way for our forces, yet for me almost alone it was a disaster and cause for grief, for it robbed me, in the very first engagement, of my husband almost before he had had time to warm himself in my embraces. I did not even succeed, as in days gone by, in capturing some prize on my own account, for my husband's untimely death prevented me from reaching the thick of the fray while booty was still to be had. All this appeared to me a certain augury of future misfortune, and for the first time in my life my spirits were oppressed with real melancholy.

After the battle the armies separated and their constituent parts set out in different directions to reconquer the lost German provinces, though they succeeded only in ruining, rather than in occupying and governing them. I for my part followed, with the regiment in which my husband had served, the host that occupied the lands about Lake Constance and the Dukedom of Württemberg, and took the opportunity of visiting the native country of my first Captain (also a gift from Prague but lost again at Hoya) and inspecting his estates. I liked his patrimony and its surroundings so well that I decided there and then to settle on it, especially since the enemies of the house of Hapsburg had been driven across the Rhine and far beyond, and so thoroughly dispersed that nothing in the world seemed more certain than that I would be safe from them here for the rest of my life. I had in any case no desire to rejoin the war, for after that famous battle of Noerdlingen there began such a ravaging of the countryside all over Germany that I doubted whether much worthwhile booty would remain for the Imperial troops.

I therefore began to lead a solid peasant's life, buying cattle and adding to the property, hiring servants and maids and behaving quite as if this one battle had put an end to the war and a peace treaty already been signed. In the same spirit I also had all my money sent to me from Prague and other large cities, and used much of it for the improvement of my estate. In fact, according to my reckoning and your memoirs, my good Simplicius, it would appear that you and I both turned to folly at about the same time: I in Swabia and you at Hanau. I wasted my money to no purpose and you your youth. You embroiled yourself in a bootless war while I vainly imagined that I lived in times of peace which, alas, were still far off. For I had scarcely struck firm roots when passing armies began once more to ravage the land and demand winter quarters, regardless of the burdensome taxes which had already taken the place of these seasonal impositions. Had I not been well supplied with money, and with wit enough to conceal it safely, it would not have been long before I was quite ruined, for no one in the town wished me well, least of all my late husband's kin, who grudged me an estate which they would otherwise have inherited if, as they put it, I had been struck by lightning as I deserved. So I was burdened with heavy taxes and yet not spared the billeting. It went with me, in short, as it commonly does with widows who are left friendless and unprotected, but I do not tell you this in a spirit of self-pity, or to enlist your comfort, help or compassion. Far from it: I would have you know that it vexed and grieved me not at all, but was, on the contrary, a cause for pleasure. Whenever I was compelled to provide winter quarters for a regiment I lost no time in making myself acquainted with the officers, and spent day and night at my house in guzzling, carousing, wenching and whoring. I let them take what liberties they liked with me, but in return made them dance to my tune afterwards, so that few of them took much money back with them from their quarters into the field. I used every trick I knew to fleece them and cared not whom it might offend. I also always employed two maids who were not a whit better than I. But so circumspect and shrewd was I in my dealings that my venerable superiors, the magistrates, found it more convenient to turn a blind eye on my exploits than to punish them, especially since as long as I was active in casting my spells, their own daughters were the less likely to fall into temptation. This life I led for several years before it turned out badly, and every springtime, when Mars took the field once again, I cast up my accounts to strike a balance of what the war had cost me during the past winter. Usually I discovered that my income had exceeded my expenditure and my prosperity increased.

And now, my good Simplicius, the time has come to tell you of the filth which I bestowed on you, for which purpose I shall interrupt my particular discourse with you and address myself to Vice, though there is nothing, of course, to prevent you from listening or, indeed, from interrupting me at will whenever you think I am lying.

Chapter Twenty-Four

WHEN the Bavarian and French armies clashed with those of the Duke of Weimar in a series of bloody skirmishes on the Swabian border, our town was heavily garrisoned, and I found plenty of officers eager for what I offered in return for the appropriate fee. But my greed for gold coupled with my insatiable natural urges tempted me to such excesses that in the end I took on all comers almost indiscriminately. And so I found myself one day with a reward which by rights I had deserved these twelve or fifteen years since: the French disease, to put it bluntly and begging the gentle reader's pardon. It caught up with me in the merry month of May. At the very moment when the earth was adorning itself with its robe of many-coloured flowers my skin erupted in pretty pustules, red as rubies, to grace my fair complexion. Fortunately I was well furnished with remedies, and retired to a town on Lake Constance for my cure. The rubies vanished in due course, but my doctor warned me that my blood was still not fully cleansed and advised me to continue my cure at the town of Griesbach with the help of mineral waters, in order to achieve a perfect recovery and be completely restored. For this purpose I equipped myself lavishly with a handsome carriage, two horses, a man-servant and a maid who was cut from precisely the same cloth and pattern as I, save that she had not yet contracted the aforementioned merry disease.

I had hardly been a week taking the waters when squire Simplicius made my acquaintance (for deep calls unto deep, as the Devil said to the charcoal-burner). I was playing my part as a lady of quality, and Simplicius, too, was cutting a dashing figure with a whole retinue of servants, so that I took him for a gallant nobleman and began to wonder whether I might not cast my rope over his horns and beguile him (as I had so many others in my time) into marrying me. It was not long before he showed himself susceptible to my charms, sailing under full canvas into the dangerous harbour of my desires, where I received him like Circe the wandering Odysseus. I was almost certain that I had him snared when the downy bird tore himself free by means of a prank which revealed his gross ingratitude, made me a public spectacle and in the end contributed to his own undoing. With a blank shot from a pistol and a clyster filled with blood which he discharged at me unawares he made me believe that I was wounded. The surgeon whom I called to dress me, and with him wellnigh the whole town, searched and examined me from top to bottom, before and behind, and when they found nothing made me the laughing-stock of Griesbach. Such a song and dance did they make about it, pointing at me and mocking me unmercifully, that in the end I could bear it no longer but left the town and its health-giving springs before my cure was completed.

Simplex, bumpkin that he is, calls me flighty in his memoirs and says that I was nubile rather than noble, both of which I admit to be true. But had he himself been of noble disposition or otherwise endowed with a shred of decency he would not have kept such intimate company with the frivolous and shameless slattern he took me for, far less proclaimed his dishonour and my shame from the roof-tops to all the world. What honour or glory can he gain, gentle reader, from having obtained (to use his own words) free access and every kind of pleasure and delight he could hope for, from a female whose easy virtue disgusted him? A female, moreover, who had not yet been properly cured of the pox! Much honour may it have done the poor devil to brag of what had best been modestly concealed. But so it goes with stallions of his ilk who, like brutish and un-reasoning beasts, hotly pursue every petticoat as a hunter does his quarry. He calls me smooth and comely, yet let me assure him that in those days I did not possess so much as the seven-teenth part of my former beauty, but was already supplement-ing it with all manner of paints and lotions, of which he collected a goodly mouthful in his slobberings. But enough of this; words are no cure for folly. Nor is the tale at an end, for I must now relate how in the end I paid him out for the mischief he did me.

I left the waters at Griesbach in high dudgeon and with the firm resolve to take my revenge. My maid had been as busy as I during our stay and, being a poor ninny with little knowledge of the world, found herself rewarded with a young son, to whom she duly gave birth at the lodge outside the town to which I had retired. I made her call the child Simplicius, though my lover of the same name had never in his life so much as touched her. As soon as I learned that the real Sim-plicius had married a peasant's daughter I had my maid wean the babe, wrap it in fine linen and lace shawls with silk ribbons and fleecy blankets, so as to give my fraud a better and more decorous appearance, and take it with one of my servants to his house, where she left it on the doorstep at dead of night, with written advice that I had got it by him. I can hardly express the delight this deception caused me, especially when I heard how suitably he was punished for it by those in authority over him, and how his wife served it up for him daily with mustard and vinegar for his supper. It also diverted me much that he was so easily persuaded that I, barren as I was, had been made pregnant by him, when his good sense should have told him that had I been capable of it I would have conceived in my youth rather than wait for him to get me with child in my approaching old age. For I was then almost forty years old. Yet even so I had not deserved a rascal as unmannerly and conceited as Simplicius.

Chapter Twenty-Five

BY rights I should now make an end and go no further with my life's story, for I have written quite enough to reveal the character of the lady whom Simplicius flatters himself to have led by the nose. But if what I have so far disclosed will surely redound only to his disgrace and shame, the sequel will bring him as little honour, and so I continue:

Behind my house in the home town of my first Captain of foot, to which I now returned, there was a garden and orchard as handsome as any in the neighbourhood. In the house next door there lived an old Peeping Tom, who had a wife even older than he. It did not take the old lecher long to discover what kind of woman I was, and I for my part did not scruple to avail myself of his services if I felt the urge or for want of anything better. So it came about that we often met in the aforesaid garden to pluck forbidden fruit in stealth and haste, for we had to take care to evade the observation of his jealous consort. Nor could we have desired a more suitable place for our encounters than the garden, whose green foliage and overhung paths concealed our wicked ways from the eyes of men, even if not from those of God—or so, at any rate, we fancied. In this, however, we erred, and those of a devout or pious disposition will conclude from what follows either that the cup of our iniquities was full to overflowing or that God in His mercy was giving us one last chance of repentance and a better life. Be that as it may, at the beginning of September we had made an assignment in the shelter of a pear tree to savour the delights of a balmy evening. But two musketeers from our garrison had chosen that very same hour to steal their portion of my pears and had already climbed the tree and started gathering the fruit when the old man and I came into the garden. It was already almost dark, and my swain was the first at the tryst. But it was not long before I joined him and we began to divert ourselves as was our habit. What happened next I do not rightly know, but I suppose one of the soldiers moved on his branch so as to get a better view of our capers, and did it so clumsily that he dropped all the pears he had already picked. As they came tumbling to the ground the old man and I had no other thought than that God had decreed and sent a violent earthquake to make us desist from our wickedness. Giving voice to these thoughts we disengaged in fear and trembling, but the two soldiers in the tree could not restrain their laughter, which greatly increased our fright, especially the Peeping Tom's, who thought a ghost had come to plague us. So we separated in the greatest confusion and each returned to the shelter of his own home.

No sooner had I reached the market next day than a musketeer shouted: 'I know something!', and another made reply equally loudly: 'Tell us then!', to which the first answered: 'There was an earthquake of pears last night.' The clamour grew apace, others taking up the tale, so that I was left in no doubt as to how matters stood and began to blush, though it was not my habit to betray confusion. It needed no gift of prophecy to foretell that I would now have to face a good harrying, though even then I did not expect it to be as fierce as it turned out. For when the children in the streets began telling of our exploits the

135

magistrates had no choice but to take me and the old Peeping Tom by the scruffs of our necks and lock us each in a separate cell, where we both denied everything like a pair of witches, though they threatened us with torture and the hangman.

They made an inventory of my possessions and impounded them, and examined my servants under oath. But their testimony was contradictory, for not all of them knew of my loose living and the maids kept faith with me. In the end it was I who settled my own hash, by putting too much trust in the mayor, who called me cousin and often visited me in prison, where he pretended to show me much kindness, though in truth he was the Law's friend rather than mine. One day he told me in confidence that the old Peeping Tom had confessed his gross and oft-repeated adultery and I, unthinking, exclaimed that I would the old shit-pot's mouth had been stuffed with hailstones since he could not keep it shut. Then I pleaded with my supposed friend to stand by me in my affliction but he, to my confusions, read me a stern lecture and then opened the door to reveal a notary and witnesses who had heard and marked all that had passed between us.

A strange trial ensued. Most of the magistrates favoured putting me to the torture, which would make me confess many more such exploits and permit them to rid the earth of a useless burden by making me shorter by a head—a sentence which was warmly commended in my presence. I, on the other hand, declared that the Court was less concerned with vindicating Justice and the Law than with confiscating my goods and chattels. If they chose to deal severely with me then many others who now were regarded as citizens of unblemished honour and good repute would be obliged to accompany me to the grave. I could hold forth like a lawyer, and my arguments were so shrewd and to the point that they impressed even men of learning. In the end it was decreed that I should be banished from the town and forfeit, as a richly deserved punishment, all my estates and movable goods, among them more than 1,000 rixdollars in ready money. My clothes and personal belongings I was allowed to take with me, except for some trinkets and jewels which had already been filched from me here and there during my imprisonment. To be brief, what was I to do? I had, after all, deserved far more severe a sentence if they had chosen to proceed against me with the full rigour of the Law. But it was a time of war and lawlessness, and so in the end all concerned could thank a kindly providence that the town and I came to so tolerable a parting of the ways.

Chapter Twenty-Six

AS it happened, there were at that time no Imperial troops or armies of any kind near enough for me to fall in with them. So for want of better employment I decided to seek out the Hessians or the Duke of Weimar's forces occupying the Kintz valley and the surrounding countryside, to see whether I could not find myself another soldier for a husband. But alas, the first flush of my incomparable beauty was now quite gone— withered away like the flowers of spring; nor had my recent misfortune and the attendant distress done anything to enhance my appearance. Riches, too, which often provide old women with husbands, I had none left. Of the clothes and trinkets I still possessed I sold whatever would fetch money, amounting altogether to some two hundred guilders, and with this and a guide I set out to seek my fortune wherever I might find it. But I encountered nothing but misfortune, for ere ever we reached their camp a patrol of Weimar musketeers set upon us, robbed, beat and chased away the guide, and carried me off with them to their quarters. I gave myself out to be the widow of an Imperial soldier whose husband had been killed at

Freiburg in Breisgau, and convinced the fellows that I had been staying in my husband's native country but was now trying to make my way back to my own home in Alsace. My looks, as I have already mentioned, were by no means what once they had been, yet they were still capable of inspiring one of my captors with enough passion to make him desire me for his wife. What choice had I? Better to surrender to this one with a good grace than to let the whole patrol rob me by force of that which he desired for love. To be brief, I became a musketeer's wife even before the chaplain had time to bless our union. I had it in mind to start up another business, as in the days of Happy-go-Lucky, but the content of my purse was unequal to the enterprise. Moreover I no longer had the help and comfort of my Bohemian mother, and also considered my husband far too coarse and feckless for such an undertaking. Nevertheless I began once more to trade in a small way in brandy and tobacco, almost as if I had wanted to recover pennywise what I had lately lost by the thousand. I found it a sore trial to be compelled to accompany the regiment on foot, and burdened with a heavy pack to boot. At times I even found myself on short commons, an experience as disagreeable to me as it was unaccustomed and, indeed, unheard of. In the end I acquired an excellent mule which could not only carry a heavier load than many a horse, but also run much faster. So now I was the proud possessor of a pair of asses, and did what I could to keep both of them in good fettle so that each might the better perform his allotted task. In this way and with my baggage no longer on my own back, I found myself more agreeably situated and content to stay where I was until, in May, we were soundly trounced by von Mercy at Herbsthausen. But before I continue with my life's story I must tell you, gentle reader, a droll adventure that befell my husband all unawares while we were in the Kitzing valley.

At the behest of his officers and with my consent he set out one day, disguised as a humble journeyman carpenter in old rags and with an axe over his shoulder, to carry some letters across country and to a destination where none could ordinarily travel for fear of roving Imperial patrols. The letters concerned the rendezvous and assembly of various forces and other plans of war. It was so bitterly cold at the time that the hand all but froze to whatever it touched, and I had it in me to pity my poor lamb of a husband. But there was no help for it, seeing that a fair sum of money was involved for us, and in the event he accomplished his task well enough. On the way back, however, he found a corpse lying across one of the secret paths by which he travelled and which he knew well. It was plainly that of an officer, for it was dressed in a pair of silver-braided scarlet officer's breeches and its ruff, boots and spurs were of the same quality. My husband examined his find and could not determine whether the fellow had frozen to death or had been murdered by the peasants of the Black Forest. But he was less concerned with the manner of his death than with his ruff, to which he took such a fancy that he stripped him of it. Having got the ruff he began to hanker after the breeches, to purloin which he must first remove the boots. This he managed easily enough, but with the breeches themselves he had more trouble. Behind the knees, where in those days they were usually laced, the moisture of the rotting body had already soaked into the lining and through to the outer cloth, so that thighs and breeches were now frozen together as hard as stone. My dolt of a husband, however, was loath to abandon the breeches, and finding, in his haste, no way of separating the flesh from the cloth he hacked off the legs above the knees with his axe, wrapped them up with the breeches and the ruff, and with this bundle was lucky enough to find shelter for the night with a peasant who gave him a place to sleep behind a warm stove.

As mischance would have it, the peasant's cow calved that very same night and the stable maid, because of the bitter cold outside, carried the calf into the room and bedded it down on a half bale of straw near the stove by my husband's side. By dawn my husband's captured breeches had thawed away from their former owner's legs, so he divested himself of some of his

140

own rags and donned the ruff and the breeches (which he had turned inside out) in their place. Then, leaving his cast-offs and the legs with the calf, he escaped through the window and made his way safely back to our lines.

A little later the stable maid returned to tend the calf, but when she saw the pair of legs together with my husband's rags and apron, and no sign of my husband himself, she began to scream like a stuck pig. She dashed from the room, slamming the door behind her as if the Devil had been at her heels, waking with her din not only the peasant, but all the neighbours as well, who thought the soldiery had descended on them, wherefore some took to their heels while the rest armed themselves for battle. The peasant, meanwhile, learned from the trembling maid the reason for her outcry: that is to say that the calf had eaten the poor carpenter they had sheltered for the night, all but the legs and feet, and that it had made so horrible a grimace at her that she was sure it was about to leap at her, too, but for the speed with which she had escaped. The peasant's first thought was to put paid to the calf with his pitchfork, but his wife would not let him venture on so perilous an enterprise or even allow him to open the door to the room. In the end she prevailed upon him to seek the Headman's assistance. The Headman straightway assembled the whole village for a massed assault on the house, so that this enemy of humankind could be dealt with and brought to judgement before it had time to grow into a cow. A diverting spectacle then ensued, with the peasant's wife handing her children and chattels out of the bedroom window one by one and the peasants peeping through the window of the chamber and gazing at the dreadful beast with the legs beside it—proof enough for them of its fearsome cruelty. Then the Headman called for an attack on the house to kill the horrible monster, but all of a sudden everyone found good reasons for saving his own skin, thinking, 'What would it profit my wife and children if I perished?' In the end a council of elders was called, and it was decided to burn down the house with the calf, whose mother mayhap had been covered by a dragon or winged serpent, and to provide the peasant with money out of the common chest to build himself another. This they proceeded to do quite merrily, comforting themselves the while with the thought that the result was no different than if it had been burnt to the ground by looting troops.

When my husband told me the tale it made me wonder whether he might not have a lucky hand for such pranks, seeing that it had all happened to him almost unawares and by chance. What might he not accomplish, I thought, if I trained him as once I did Happy-go-Lucky? But the booby was far too dull and timid; moreover I soon lost him in the encounter at Herbsthausen, where he met his end just because he was no match for a resolute adversary.

Chapter Twenty-Seven

FROM this battle I escaped with the help of my good mule, abandoning my tent and the lesser part of my baggage. Together with the remnants of the army and Turenne himself I withdrew to Cassel, and since my husband was dead and I now quite friendless and forsaken, I sought refuge at last with the gipsies who accompanied Koenigsmark's forces, which were part of the main Swedish army that had joined us at Wartburg. Their leader was a one-time Lieutenant who soon became aware of my several virtues: my skill at thieving, the small sum of money I still possessed and other qualities of the same kind which recommended me to the tribe. And so, almost before I knew where I was, I had become his wife, an arrangement which had this advantage at least: that henceforth I had no further need of powder, pomades and ointments to make myself white and beautiful. Both my new station in life and my husband demanded of me that colour which they called the Devil's livery, wherefore they proceeded to anoint me with goose-dripping, louse-oil and various unguents for changing the colour of the hair, so that in no time at all I acquired as hellish a complexion as if I had been born in the very heart of Egypt. Whenever I looked in a mirror I could not help laughing at my reflection and marvelling at my complete transformation. But for all that I found the gipsy life so much to my taste that I would not have changed places with a Colonel's wife. From an old Egyptian grandmother I soon learned the art of sooth-saying; of lessons in lying, cheating and thieving I had no need, though the gipsies knew a trick or two that were new even to me. But what matter? I soon learned them so perfectly that I could easily have passed as the supreme commander and captain-in-chief of all the gipsies.

Yet though I made more booty for my husband to squander on liquor and revelry than any ten others of my ilk, I was not so accomplished a felon as to escape all perils and even some rude buffets, as the following story will show. On the march we camped for a day and a night near an allied town, which all might enter to make whatever small purchases they fancied. I, too, made my way there, though for the purpose of thieving and of making rather than spending money, for I had no intention of taking anything back but what my wits or the skill of my fingers might secure for me free of charge. I had not penetrated far into the town before a young lady sent me her maid to ask for her fortune to be told. By dint of discreet inquiries on our way to the house I discovered from the maid that her mistress' lover had turned fickle and was bestowing his favours elsewhere. This intelligence stood me in excellent stead when I met the lady, and my predictions proved so much to the point and to her liking that the poor innocent thought them superior to all her almanacks and the writ of the holy prophets themselves. She ended by telling me of all her troubles and besought me to use whatever means I knew to bewitch her faithless lover and restore him to her arms. 'Indeed, fair lady,' I said, 'he shall be compelled to turn from his waywardness and be restored to you, even though he were as well armed against secret charms as the great Goliath himself.' This assurance was music to the poor lovesick ninny's ears, and nothing would satisfy her but that I should put my great art to the test there and then. I advised her that we must not be overheard and that everything must be done in the greatest secrecy. So she dismissed her maids and swore them to absolute discretion. Then the two of us repaired to her bedchamber, where I asked her for a black veil she had worn in mourning for her father, a pair of ear-rings, a precious necklace she was wearing, her gold-embroidered belt and her lover's ring. When I had taken possession of these jewels I wrapped them in the veil, knotted it in various places, mumbling strange and meaningless incantations the while, and finally placed the package on her bed. Then I told her that we must go down to the cellar together, and when we got there persuaded her to undress down to her shift while I drew some magic designs on the side of a large barrel of wine. Finally I withdrew the spigot from the barrel and ordered the lady to put her finger in the bung-hole while I went back upstairs to perform my magic with the spigot. Having tethered the poor lamb in this manner I went to collect the jewels and ran out of town as quickly as my feet would carry me.

But whether this pious and gullible young lover enjoyed a special protection from on high or whether it was just not written in my stars that I should have her jewels, at any rate I was stopped well before I had reached safety by a cavalier who was an officer of the garrison and ordered me to return my loot. Though I swore to high heaven that I had nothing to surrender, he soon proved me a liar. For when he ordered his servant to dismount and search me, and I whipped out my wicked gipsy knife to prevent it, the officer drew his sword, and with the flat of it belaboured my head, shoulders, sides and buttocks so unmercifully that I was a full month nursing the bruises. I do believe the devil would not have left off beating me to this day had I not at last thrown my prize at his feet. And so, for once, honest love and cunning fraud both earned their just reward.

Chapter Twenty-Eight

NOT long after I had weathered this encounter our tribe of gipsies drifted away from Koenigsmark's troops to return to the main Swedish army as it moved into Bohemia under Torstensohn's command, where the two finally joined forces. With this army I remained until the end of the war, accompanied always by my faithful mule, and thereafter, when peace had returned, could not find it in my heart to forsake the gipsies, for by then the habit of thieving had become second nature to me. And as I perceive that my scribe still has a blank page of paper left I will make him fill it, by way of farewell, with a final prank. The idea of it came to me but recently and was tested on the spot. It will serve to show you, gentle reader, how I persisted in my old ways, and will help you to guess what I accomplished in the interval and how well suited I was with the gipsies.

We were in Lorraine at the time, and at nightfall came upon a large village where they were holding their church fair. For this reason, and because there were a goodly number of us— men, women, children and horses—they flatly refused us shelter for the night. But my husband, calling himself

147

Lieutenant-Colonel, pledged his word as a nobleman that he would stand surety for any damage and make good out of his own pocket whatever might be spoilt or stolen, and to mete out severe punishment where necessary. On these terms, and after much parleying, they finally made us welcome. The place was so full of the delicious odours of festival fare that it soon whetted my appetite and made me grumble that the peasants should be the only ones to enjoy what was everywhere cooking, baking and frying. I quickly hatched a plan that would enable us all to have our share, and to set it in train got one of our staunchest young lads to shoot a chicken straight in front of the village inn, where the deed would be sure to cause the greatest stir. At once my husband was assailed by angry villagers clamouring for redress. He made a great show of anger and ordered a fellow whom we had with us as trumpeter to sound the assembly. While peasants and gipsies gathered on the green I moved about among them, telling our folk in our thieves' tongue what my plan was and warning the women to be ready to pounce. My husband briefly sat in judgement over the culprit and condemned him to be hanged for having disobeyed his orders. Immediately the word went round the village that the Lieutenant-Colonel was having a gipsy hanged for so paltry a thing as a dead chicken, which some thought too severe a punishment while others praised him for keeping such good order. One of our troop played the part of hangman and set about tying the malefactor's hands behind his back. One of the gipsy women pretended to be the condemned man's wife, and with three children she had quickly borrowed for the purpose, came running on the scene to plead for the life of her husband and the father of her tender brood with so convincing a show of despair that it would have wrung tears from a stone. But my husband, deaf and blind to her entreaties, waited until he reckoned that the whole village had forgathered to see the poor sinner hanged, before having him taken to a nearby wood for the execution of the sentence. And indeed, almost the whole village, old and young, men, women, children and servants, all followed the procession. Meanwhile the young gipsy woman with her three children never ceased weeping, wailing and begging for mercy, and when they reached the tree in the wood where the deed was to be done she was in so pitiful a state that first the peasant women and then even their menfolk began to plead for the wretched chicken-slayer and would not be appeased until at last my husband relented and agreed to a reprieve for their sakes.

While we were performing this comedy outside the village, our womenfolk, who had remained behind, were filling their pockets at leisure, taking not only what was cooking and broiling, but also anything else of value that they could lay their hands on. When they had done, they came out to join us, as if to stir up their menfolk against me and my husband for our cruelty in wanting to hang a decent lad for the sake of a mangy old hen, leaving his poor wife a widow and his innocent children orphaned. But in our own language they told us that they had made a good killing with which we had better be on our way before the peasants discovered their loss. So I called out to some of our men that they should feign a rebellion and pretend to flee deeper into the wood. My husband and those about him made as if to pursue them with swords drawn and even firing their muskets after them, though with no thought of doing them any harm. The peasants took fright at the impending massacre, as they imagined it, and hastened back to their homes, but we continued to pursue each other, firing as we went, ever deeper into the forest where we were familiar with every stick and stone. In short, we marched all through the night, and next morning divided the spoils and went our separate ways in small groups, thus avoiding all danger of pursuit by the peasants.

With this tribe of gipsies have I wandered these many years now over the length and breadth of Europe, hatching, planning and executing so many plots and tricks on the way that a whole ream of paper would scarcely suffice to tell of them all. And it has puzzled me beyond measure all my life that so many

149

peoples have suffered us to dwell among them. For we disdain to be of use or service to either God or man, seeking only to make our living by lies, fraud and theft to the damage both of peasants and nobles, whose venison we consume in great quantities. But of this I must say no more for fear of bringing us into even worse odour. In any event I am content to have said enough for the eternal discomfiture of Simplicius, who boasted so bravely to all and sundry of the fine concubine he had while taking the waters at Griesbach. Moreover I suspect that his other gallant conquests may not have been so very different, and that more often than not he fell into the toils of French whores or even witches, which would at least make him brother-in-law to the Devil.

Postscript by the Author

WHEREFORE, ye chaste youths, honest widowers and married men to boot, ye who have hitherto warded off these dangerous Chimeras, averted your eyes from these horrible Medusas, stopped up your ears against these accursed Sirens and renounced these unfathomable and abysmal Beldams, or at any rate escaped them by flight; continue also in future to resist their blandishments, for nothing is more certain than that a whore's love will lead only to filth, shame, mockery, corruption and misery and, above all, to an uneasy conscience. It is then that we perceive what it has profited us, how revolting, shameless, lousy, scurvy, unclean, stinking both of breath and body they have been, putrefied inside by the pox and outside by boils so that in the end, though, alas, too late, nothing is left but remorse.